STO

ALASKAN SUMMER

ALASKAN SUMMER

by
Mary Collins Dunne

Illustrated by
Elisabeth Grant

Abelard-Schuman
London · New York · Toronto

London	*New York*	*Toronto*
Abelard-Schuman	Abelard-Schuman	Abelard-Schuman
Limited	Limited	Canada Limited
8 King St. WC2	6 West 57th St.	1680 Midland Ave.

Printed in the United States of America

1693946

Dedicated to My Family

All characters in the book are fictitious.
These places in the book are fictitious: Otsego Falls,
Pine Center, Winona, Crescent Valley, Rekova
Valley, town of Rekova, Wolverine River, Honak
River, Setnek.

Contents

1
OFF TO ALASKA

Mark Bennett stood by the window in the early June dusk. He was a big, light-haired boy, tall for twelve, with shoulders that filled his tan jacket.

"Lynn!" he called. "It's time to leave."

"In a minute," came a voice from the back porch. "I'm saying good-bye to Juju." Juju was the black and white mother cat who belonged to the Wilsons next door. Seven-year-old Lynn was on close terms with every pet in the neighborhood.

Mark gazed down the tree-lined street. What a pretty town Otsego Falls was. Probably the nicest in all of northern inland Washington. Lights began to flick on in the homes beyond the well-kept lawns and gardens. A feeling of sadness gripped the boy. He turned and gazed at the empty room. The whole house was bare now.

How fast it all had happened. Two weeks ago, Grandma's warm, cheery presence had filled this place. Now she was gone, and the house was being sold. Strangers would move into the home where Mark and his sister had lived ever since their mother's death five years before.

Warmhearted neighbors had been kind to the Bennetts these past weeks, but Mark still felt numb and dazed. This automobile trip to Alaska seemed unreal too — the journey on which he and Lynn were to embark tonight with people they had never even met.

But Dad would be waiting at the end of the long trip. Mark's spirits rose. Dad, with his quick smile and steady eyes. Mark hadn't seen his father since Dad had been home on military leave last year. The boy's thoughts leaped ahead to the end of July, when the Alaskan vacation would be over, and his father would be out of the service for good. They would all return to Otsego Falls together, Mark thought happily. He remembered a vacant house he had seen with a "For Rent" sign on it, the Hart place, at the edge of town. It would be just big enough for the three of them. He pictured the windows of the Hart house all golden with lights, *their* lights. It gave him a warm feeling. Yes, he would tell his father about the Hart house the first thing.

Lynn came into the room holding Sally Sue, the big rag doll from whom she was seldom separated. Grandma had made the doll for Lynn's last birthday, embroidering every stitch with loving care. Sally Sue had shell-pink cloth skin and yellow wool hair tied into braids, and her red mouth always smiled. The doll was more than just a toy to Lynn — it was a precious keepsake.

"Where did you say the Wilsons were going to drive us?" Lynn asked.

"To the junction, where the caravan will stop for the night."

Mark and his sister looked alike, with straw-colored hair and wide blue eyes. Freckles, like specks of cinnamon, were sprinkled across their noses. But while Mark was big and loose-limbed, Lynn was small-boned and dainty-looking, an appearance that belied her tomboy traits.

Mark put their suitcases on the front porch and whistled for Stormy, the faithful big German shepherd who had been with them since he was a fur ball of a puppy. They had already said all their good-byes around town. With the dog beside them, they walked next door and rang the bell.

The door opened, and a sudden chorus of voices sang out from the Wilson's living room. "Surprise!"

Mark's breath caught in his throat as a laughing group milled around him and Lynn, pulling them inside. All their friends and neighbors. He'd never expected this!

"We couldn't let you leave without a little send-off," declared Mrs. Wilson, from the dining room, where she was cutting a big fudge cake.

Jeff's mother was busily serving out mounds of cherry-studded vanilla ice cream.

"Some going-away presents." Mr. Wilson smiled as he thrust a stack of gaily wrapped packages at the surprised Bennetts. Lynn's eyes sparkled with excitement as she unwrapped some of them. "Oh, look, Mark! Cookies, and a big box of candy."

"Books," Mark breathed, gazing at his opened gifts.

"Games, stationery." As he and Lynn thanked everyone, happiness warmed Mark's heart. How thoughtful and kind these people were.

His Madison School classmates clustered around — Allan, Jeff, the whole gang, even Rich, the new boy on the block. What a good group of friends. Chuck Wilson squeezed onto the sofa beside Mark — Chuck, the best pal a fellow could ever have. Mark would miss Chuck for the next month. They were like brothers, in and out of each other's homes every day, doing things together for years.

The hum of voices rose and fell. Rich leaned toward Mark. "How long has your father been stationed in Alaska?"

Mark swallowed a mouthful of Mrs. Wilson's delicious cake. "Two years. He's getting out of the army in July."

"Why didn't he — ?" Rich blurted out. Then he paused, embarrassed.

Mark put down his fork. "You're wondering why my father didn't fly home when Grandma died." His tone was sober. "I know he must have felt bad about not being here for the funeral. But he's been recovering from his appendicitis operation. He couldn't possibly travel."

"Is he all right now?" Rich asked.

"He's coming along okay. By the time we get there, he'll be pretty well."

Mr. Wilson spoke up. "When Lieutenant Bennett heard about the car caravan that would pass near here on its way to Alaska, he arranged for Mark and Lynn to travel with it."

"Dad wrote that he had a surprise waiting for us,"

Mark said. "I bet it's a hunting trip up there, as soon as he's better. That will really be something, won't it?"

"Boy, I'll say!" Mark's friends agreed. "Camping in those big mountains." "Maybe a riverboat trip."

"But hurry back, Mark," Chuck put in. "We have to keep up our baseball practice. The Otters would be sunk next season without our star pitcher." Chuck grinned. "The great, the fabulous, the one and only Mark Bennett."

Mark smiled. He knew that underneath the kidding Chuck really meant it. Mark's tricky curve ball had been worth all the practice he'd given it. The Madison School baseball team depended mainly on Mark's strikes to knock out their rival batters. "I'm taking my glove," he said. "Dad will help me to keep in practice."

"More cake, Mark?"

"M-mm, thanks." Chuck's mother slid another wedge of chocolate cake onto his plate.

"I read a newspaper article about the seven families in this auto caravan," Mr. Wilson said. "Twenty-eight persons in all, from Washington and Oregon. Some are experienced farmers and dairymen; others are beginners. They're going to claim homesteads in Alaska and make their living from the soil."

Jeff was puzzled. "I thought Alaska was too cold to grow anything."

"Me, too," echoed several other boys.

"Some parts are," Mr. Wilson told them. "But during the short summer, crops can be raised and herds grazed in certain places. The Matanuska Valley, near Anchorage, in south-central Alaska, is a fertile area. Also the Tanana Valley, in the interior part of the state, near Fairbanks. There are others, just waiting to be developed. These homesteaders look upon Alaska as a place of challenge and opportunity."

"Like settlers in covered wagons, coming west in the old days," Chuck mused.

Mrs. Wilson nodded. "These people are modern pioneers. I read about them, too. They're going to cultivate soil that has never known a plow before. They'll build their houses of logs from trees they've chopped down themselves."

Modern pioneers. It would be exciting to travel with them, but Mark was glad that he and Lynn were only tourists.

All at once, it was time for good-byes. The Bennetts were to join the caravan at the junction five miles beyond town. Everyone swarmed down the front steps as Mr. Wilson put the luggage and gifts into the car. Mrs. Wilson, who had looked after Mark and Lynn for the past two weeks, hugged the little girl. Then she clasped Mark's hand. "Remember us to your father, Mark."

Lynn's friends circled around like chattering blue jays. The mild June twilight rang with their calls.

" 'Bye, Lynn! 'Bye!"

Even Juju, the cat, rubbed against Lynn's legs for one last petting.

"See you in August!" Jeff shouted.

Mark leaned from the car window, shaking hands,

promising himself that he would bring Alaskan souvenirs to them all.

Chuck Wilson. hopped into the car beside Stormy. Mark waved until they turned the corner. Then he sat back, holding his camera.

"You youngsters are lucky to be going on this grand trip to the largest state," Mr. Wilson said, as they drove out to the highway. "Do you know that Alaska is one-fifth the size of these forty-eight states? That's really big."

Mark tried to picture its vastness, but his eyes were on the tall evergreens growing on every side, casting stately shadows against the evening sky.

"Hey, Stormy, what'll you do when you see your first moose or bear?" Chuck affectionately pulled the dog's ears.

"Lucky we could bring old Storm with us," Mark said.

Soon they reached the junction where the caravan from southern Washington had stopped on the first lap of its long journey. Mark looked around with great interest as Mr. Wilson parked the car. The caravan vehicles were stopped in a quiet, wooded spot with a small clearing. Mark saw one house trailer and a pickup truck, two campers, three big-bodied automobiles and a station wagon, each with a hauling trailer. The families apparently had just finished their evening meal. A few sleeping tents were set up. A small group of men relaxed on camp chairs and logs, talking in the summer dimness. Another group sat in the glow of a gasoline lantern, leaning over maps that were spread out before them. Women were busy tidying up dishes and utensils, while small children frolicked in and out of the trees.

Stormy sniffed around, pricking up his ears at the sound of a bark within the camp. As Stormy answered the bark with increasing excitement, Mark held the dog's collar.

A pleasant, gray-haired man came forward to greet the newcomers. "Hello, there. I'm Dan Towers, in charge of the caravan. Are these our new members?"

"Yes, sir. I'm Mark Bennett, and this is my sister, Lynn." Mark introduced Mr. Wilson and Chuck.

A tall, smiling man joined Mr. Towers. He was followed by a little boy in Levis and a plaid shirt. "George Bennett's children?" the tall man inquired. "I'm John Hillman. This is my son, Tim. Your father wrote to me. A cousin of mine, on a trip to Fairbanks, had told him about us and our caravan. In my answer, I promised that you could ride with us." He shook Mark's and Lynn's hands.

Mark liked Mr. Hillman at once. There was a friendliness about him that put Mark at his ease. The little boy Tim, after an alert appraisal of the Bennetts, turned his attention to their dog.

Mark and Lynn bade Mr. Wilson good-bye. "A pleasant trip!" he wished them all. Mark walked to their car. He gripped Chuck's hand tightly. "Have fun," Chuck said, "and take care of that famous pitching arm."

"So long, Chuck." Mark watched his pal climb back into the car. If only Chuck could have come along! Mark waved steadily until the Wilsons' car was out of sight.

"Nice dog, good dog." Stormy wagged a friendly tail as Tim Hillman petted him.

"His name is Stormy." Mark smiled at the small,

bright-eyed boy whose closely cropped hair stood up
stiff as a wire brush. "We called him that because when
we first saw him, he looked gray and dark like a lot of
storm clouds."

Suddenly, Stormy growled. A smooth-haired, brown
dog with white paws was circling him, rumbling low in
his throat. Stormy barked sharply, and again Mark
seized the dog's collar. The smaller dog barked, too,
and then stood still, as though uncertain of his next
move.

"Pandowdy!" It was the voice of Mr. Towers, the
gray-haired leader of the caravan. He grabbed his dog's
collar. "These two will have to learn how to get along
with each other."

"Pandowdy. What a crazy name for a dog!" Lynn
exclaimed.

"Lynn!" Mark reprimanded. She was so outspoken.

But Mr. Towers smiled. "I'll tell you how he got the
name, honey. One day when he was a pup, my wife
made apple pandowdy and set it on the kitchen window-
sill to cool. Well, that puppy had a sweet tooth. He
reached it on a nearby chair and cleaned up the whole
panful."

Mark and Lynn laughed. "Does he still like it?" Lynn
asked.

Mr. Towers shook his head. "He's never had anymore
since then. My wife cools it in a safe place now." He
looked at Stormy. "That's a nice-looking dog, good blood
lines. I'm afraid Pandowdy's a bit of every breed, but
he's a loyal little mongrel."

"Stormy's friendly," Mark told him. "I think once they
get acquainted they'll be all right."

"Come along and meet the other folks," Mr. Hillman said. He led Mark and Lynn through the camp, with Tim importantly holding onto Stormy's collar. The pleasing aroma of the pines mingled with the crisp smell of campfire smoke upon the night air. Stars dotted the clear sky, and the yellow moon had begun to rise.

As Mark met the other families, he was disappointed not to see any boys his own age. But the people were so friendly that this long trip with strangers, about which he'd felt anxious, took on a bright outlook.

2
CARAVANS NORTH

"Come along! You've met everyone except the rest of my family," Mr. Hillman called out to the Bennetts. His tan station wagon was parked a little distance away. Mrs. Hillman, a pretty woman with fair, silky hair, was getting a pink-faced baby girl ready for bed. She greeted the Bennetts warmly. Donna, the baby, pointed to Lynn's doll and chattered in delight.

"Here. Want to hold it?" Lynn offered. Donna hugged the doll, which was almost as big as she was.

"Such a pretty gingham dress your doll has," Mrs. Hillman remarked.

"My grandma made her wardrobe," Lynn confided. She opened a little trunk that was set on top of their luggage. "See this little hand-knitted sweater and the blue coat with the white fur collar."

Donna suddenly let the doll slide from her arms as her attention switched to Stormy, with whom her brother Tim was playing. " 'Tormy!" she excitedly repeated after him.

"She means Stormy," Tim explained. "She can't say *s* yet."

Lynn helped Mark unpack their boxes of candy and cookies, which they shared with the Hillmans. "Donna, next time aim for your mouth," Mr. Hillman said with a laugh, as he wiped chocolate from his small daughter's face. One blob even decorated her button nose.

"Tim, will you help us to pass some of this among the other people?" Mark asked.

They went through camp offering the sweets to the caravan members. When they came back to the Hillman camp, little Donna, in yellow pajamas with a scottie dog print, was being put to bed in the back of the station wagon. "Hi, 'tormy boy, 'tormy girl," she chattered.

"Their names are Mark and Lynn, not Stormy's boy and girl," Tim told her, but it was plain that Donna thought Stormy was the most important one.

"She loves that dog," Mrs. Hillman said. Donna gazed at Stormy, and his brown eyes seemed to reflect her affectionate look.

"If it's all right with you," Mark said to Mrs. Hillman, "Stormy could sleep by her feet, there at the end of the station wagon."

Donna squealed and clapped her hands. Mrs. Hillman laughed. "Donna's in favor of your idea, Mark."

At a word from Mark, Stormy jumped in and lay at the feet of his new little admirer, who soon seemed to be sound asleep. Mark set down a half-filled box of chocolate creams. "Let me help you." he gave Mr. Hillman a hand unrolling the five sleeping bags in which they were to sleep on the ground. Then they inflated the air mattresses and set the bags on top of them.

"I want to go to bed," Lynn decided, eager to try this new outdoor sleeping. She changed in the little dressing tent and snuggled into her bag. In a matter of minutes, she was asleep, with her rag doll's unblinking face beside her own.

"Lynn must have been tired," Mrs. Hillman said, smoothing a strand of blond hair from the little girl's cheek. "I suppose it's been a busy day for both of you."

Mark nodded. But he was too excited to go to bed.

"Would you like to see our route on the map?" Mr. Hillman asked him. "Come along with us."

Mark eagerly followed Mr. and Mrs. Hillman and Tim over the soft pine needles to Mr. Towers' camp, where a gasoline lantern glowed brightly. Pandowdy dozed under a tree, his head upon his white forepaws. Mrs. Towers, a plump, silvery-haired woman with gentle eyes, set out folding stools for the visitors.

Mark looked with interest at the big road map Dan Towers opened out. "How long will this trip take?" Mark asked.

"About eight days if we make three hundred miles a day. Look, here we are in northern Washington. See our route?" All heads bent over the map as the caravan leader traced the thin red line of the Cariboo Highway through British Columbia. "There are lots of mountains," Dan Towers said, "with curves to slow us down. But we'll make the best time we can. See the town of Dawson Creek, 'way up here in Canada?" Mark peered where Mr. Towers pointed, to a circle near the British Columbia—Alberta border. "That's where we get on our main road, the Alaska Highway."

Mark was surprised to see that the Alaska Highway traveled about as far west as it did north. Then he remembered learning at school that the Alaskan cities of Anchorage and Fairbanks were located almost as far westward as the Hawaiian Islands.

"We've picked a good time of year to travel up there," Mr. Towers continued. "June weather is comfortable, about 75 degrees in the daytime, 35 at night."

"I've heard that the highway is very dusty," Mrs. Hillman said.

"It used to be, at certain seasons, but it's not so bad anymore." Dan Towers shook his head. "I was talking to a fellow who drove down not long ago. He said that all of the Alaskan part and some of the Canadian part are blacktopped, paved with asphalt. The rest is a well-ballasted gravel surface. There are precautions we can take if we hit dusty stretches. And, of course, there might be rain."

Mr. Hillman turned to Mark. "Dan worked on the Alaska Highway when it was being built. During the Second World War, wasn't it, Dan?"

"That's right, in '42 and '43. It was called the Alcan then."

"I remember that time well," Mrs. Towers recalled. "All the wives were waiting at home. The highway was supposed to take two years to build, but they finished it in only eight months."

Dan Towers gazed far beyond the campfire. "Never have I seen such determined, hard-working men. Army engineers, battalions of soldiers — I was one of them — thousands of civilian workers. And what land we had to combat! Every possible kind except desert."

Mark leaned forward with interest. What a challenge it must have been to build a road through stark wilderness. "I bet there were mountains."

"No less than five high ranges. And there were thick forests, one after another. Rivers — talk about rivers! — there must have been two hundred of them, big and small. And to crown it all, there were miles and miles of dangerous muskeg."

"What's muskeg, Mr. Towers?"

"Treacherous stuff, let me tell you. It's swamp bogs formed in drained lake and river beds, from 5 to 40 feet deep. In summer it's so soggy it won't even hold the weight of a log. Once, I saw a bulldozer disappear into the muskeg for keeps. Luckily, the driver jumped free in time and was saved by his fellow workers."

"The engineers and workers had trouble with weather, too, didn't they?" Mr. Hillman asked.

"And how! Bitter cold in winter; rain, mud and flash floods in spring. Then summer brought humid heat and swarms of pesky insects. Oh, those mosquitoes were a scourge!" Mr. Towers held up his hands. "But nothing stopped the building of the 'lifeline to the north'— over 1,500 miles long. Later, the highway was widened and improved, with steel bridges replacing the original log ones."

Mark could have stayed all night, listening to the caravan master's conversation, but after the grown-ups had finished their coffee and Mark and Tim their mugs of cocoa, they all said "Good night." Mark followed the path the Hillmans' flashlight cut through the dark, quiet camp. Mr. Hillman shone the beam for a moment on the slumbering Lynn, then on Donna and Stormy.

"Oh, no!" Mrs. Hillman gave a smothered gasp.

Mark followed her gaze to the station wagon. Stormy lay there, awake and alert. Donna slept, curled up in a ball. But what —? Mark leaned forward to look more closely at her face. It was smeared to the eyes with chocolate. Beside her lay the telltale empty box, with little brown pleated paper circles strewn around.

"I thought she was fast asleep when we left." Her father shook his head.

"I left the candy here," Mark recalled. "I never thought —"

"It's not your fault." Mrs. Hillman patted his arm. "She's an imp! Imagine her devouring all your candy. Look, she tried to share some with your dog." She sighed as she tucked in the small culprit. "I'm afraid she won't feel very well tomorrow."

As soon as Mark wriggled into his sleeping bag, drowsiness overtook him. The last thing he remembered was the smell of evergreens and the sight of stars that winked at him through the lacy branches.

Morning sounds awakened Mark, and he squinted at the bright sunshine. Mr. and Mrs. Hillman, in gaily printed sport shirts, were busy at the camp stove. The delicious aroma of bacon wafted over to Mark. Lynn stirred and then sat halfway up. Tim, already dressed, played a lively chasing game with Stormy. Mark heard a whimper from the station wagon. Then he saw Donna's tousled head emerging from the bedclothes. Her scrubbed little face looked pale and doleful.

"You had a bad time with that old upset tummy, didn't you? Her mother stroked Donna's forehead. "Here, honey, drink this."

All of them except Donna ate a good breakfast, waving greetings to nearby families. Afterward, the children divided up tasks that had to be done. Lynn tried to amuse Donna, who was cross and irritable. Tim helped his mother to put away food and to dry dishes. Mark and Mr. Hillman rolled up the sleeping gear and packed it in the hauling trailer.

Dan Towers came along with instructions for the day. "We want to make the town of Pine Center in British Columbia by tonight," Mark heard him say to Mr. Hillman. They would cross over into Canada today, Mark realized with mounting excitement.

"All aboard!" Mr. Hillman called out. They took their places in the station wagon. Soon, the whole caravan was ready to leave. The vehicles moved out, turning into the main highway. Traffic was light as they traveled steadily toward the Canadian border. Wispy white clouds floated across the blue sky. Sunshine washed over distant mountains in a golden wave. By midmorning, the caravan had reached the international border at Winona, the port of entry. Mark felt excited. He had never been in Canada before. He got out Stormy's veterinary certificate to have it ready. Mr. Wilson had told him that animals must be proven free from disease before being allowed to cross the border. "Do you have to pay duty on anything?" he asked the Hillmans.

"No. Our personal belongings can be carried duty free," Mr. Hillman replied. "And passports aren't required of United States citizens."

They lined up for customs, inching forward little by little. Tim rolled down his window as they drew near to the customs man. "Do any Northwest Mounties ride

their horses around here?" he asked hopefully. "I saw them in movies lots of times."

The man smiled, pausing briefly in his work. "No more horses, young fellow. The Royal Canadian Mounted Police use pickup trucks and airplanes nowadays. And don't expect to see them wearing red. That's only for dress affairs."

"Aw, gee." Tim was disappointed. But he brightened up to hear that in deep winter snow some of the Mounties used dog teams for travel.

The families moved along, one by one. Soon all the homesteaders had gone through customs. The caravan moved onward again, heading north through British Columbia. Looking out of the window, Mark wondered how he and his father and sister would come back. Probably by plane. Dad would want to get back home to Otsego Falls the quickest way possible.

The sky gradually became overcast as masses of rolling gray clouds blotted out the sun. Mr. Hillman tried to get a weather report on the radio, but all that emerged was the sound of crackling static. The road was mountainous, filled with sudden curves and sharp turns. Mr. Hillman drove with great care. Donna, ill and cranky, slept fitfully on her mother's lap. During the afternoon, Tim and Lynn dozed off, too. As the day wore on, the threatening weather cleared.

Toward nightfall, the caravan began to look for a good camping spot, level, unfenced and free of "No Trespassing" signs. As twilight shadows colored the mountains purple, Mr. Towers found a place outside the tiny town of Pine Center. All the homesteaders followed his car into a side road, which led to a meadow.

How good it felt to get out and stretch cramped muscles. Stormy and Pandowdy, after a few growls at each other, bounded around exuberantly at sight of some rabbits in the grass. The wild creatures easily eluded the noisy, town-raised dogs. Everyone was hungry and felt glad to hear that campfires would be allowed, since Mr. Towers had obtained a fire permit.

Mark noted the care that was taken with each family's fire. Inflammable material — mosses, dry undergrowth — — was scraped into a 6-foot circle before the fire was built.

Among their supplies, the families had brought canned and packaged foods and some fruits and vegetables that would keep well. Lynn helped Mrs. Hillman to scrub big potatoes and to wrap them in aluminum foil. The potatoes were placed, along with covered ears of corn, to roast beneath the embers. Patties of frozen chopped beef, bought in Winona, had thawed out for perfect broiling. Mark decided he had never tasted better food than that meal under the starry Canadian skies. After supper, Mark helped Mr. Hillman to douse the fire with water. They stirred the ashes into mud and then covered that with earth.

The homesteaders all had a good night's rest. Early next morning, the women joined forces to make a hearty breakfast of griddle cakes with syrup. How delicious the pancakes tasted in the nippy dawn. As the caravan drove away from Pine Center, dewdrops still clung like pearls to leaves and grasses. Mark watched the sky gradually turn from soft gray to pink, pale as the inside of a shell. Then the pink grew rosier, chasing away the last shadow of night, and the sun came up in a brilliant golden ball.

All day, they had pleasant weather for their journey as they traveled northward through magnificent mountains. Every now and then, Mrs. Hillman brought out a simple game or crayons and hard-cover coloring books for the restless Tim and Lynn. She sang soothing lullabies to little Donna, who was her happy, apple-cheeked self again.

The caravan turned east into the prairies. "This is wheat country." Mr. Hillman pointed to huge red grain elevators near railroad tracks. "As well as being good for farming, this area is rich in minerals, oil and natural gas. Next stop, Dawson Creek. That's where we'll change to the Alaska Highway. Remember?"

When the homesteaders reached the bustling town of Dawson Creek, they turned into the free public campground for an overnight stay. After they had freshened up, Mark went with the men to buy supplies — "We mustn't forget mosquito-repellent lotion!" Dan Towers advised — while the women took advantage of a modern launderette they'd seen in town, to assure a supply of clean clothes.

Then the men got their vehicles ready for the main part of their trip. Gasoline tanks were covered with rubber matting to protect them from flying gravel. Masking tape was applied to keep dust out of the trunks. They put plastic shields on the headlights and insect screens in front of the radiators.

Mark watched these preparations with rising excitement. Tomorrow, they would be on the Alaska Highway, the "lifeline to the north."

3

THROUGH THE MOUNTAINS

Early next morning, the caravan got started. As they drove out of town, they slowed down to gaze at the big milepost that said "Mile O."

"Fairbanks, 1523," Mark read, and his heart beat faster. Every mile of this long road would bring him and Lynn closer to their father. They turned into the Alaska Highway and soon drove through a section of fertile farmlands.

"Hey, look at the big bridge!" Tim and Lynn grew excited as they approached the wide Peace River.

"I heard that this bridge was built around 1960," Mrs. Hillman said, "to replace a suspension bridge that had gradually collapsed."

Mark had read some of the history of the region. "They say that this river got its name from being a boundary of truce between the warring Cree and Beaver Indians."

"This area has a colorful past," Mr. Hillman agreed. "In early days the Peace River was the scene of the fur-trade traffic. Big canoes of the Hudson Bay and other companies used to bring out the valuable furs."

Soon, the caravan passed through a town named Fort St. John. The cars kept at "dust distance" from each other. They left the farm country and entered a region of wilderness. It was full of untouched forests and swift streams, with the great Canadian Rockies in the background. Mark thought again of the strong brave men, like Dan Towers, who had carved this road through such a rugged land. Now at intervals there were cafés, motels and auto shops, as well as maintenance and power stations with telephone service.

The homesteaders met other motorists going north in all sorts of vehicles. One family rode in a made-over school bus; many traveled in campers. Some cars were leaving the north country, heading for Dawson Creek. The caravan slowly climbed up Trutch Mountain, whose elevation of 4,000 feet disclosed a series of panoramic views. Streaks of clouds looked like blurred chalk smudges against the blue sky.

"Want to get some pictures?" Mr. Hillman slowed down so that Mark could take snapshots.

As the day passed, Mark did not want to miss any of the sights, but the car's motion on the winding road lulled him. In spite of himself, he dozed off, awakening when they had almost reached Fort Nelson, where they were going to spend the night.

"The post office name of this little town is Muskwa," Mrs. Hillman read from her travel folder. "That means *bear*, and it says that there are lots of bear around here."

"I hope we see some!" Tim exclaimed.

"Maybe they'll come around when we're eating supper," Lynn said hopefully.

"If they do," Mrs. Hillman smiled, "don't argue with them over the food."

The grimy vehicles that pulled to a stop did not look much like the polished cars of a few days ago. The travelers, too, were dusty and weary, but cheerful that this much of the journey was now behind them.

Mark was interested to discover that such small Canadian towns had airports. "Air travel is common in the north where distances are so vast," Mr. Hillman told him.

Dan Towers smiled at Lynn as Pandowdy nuzzled against her. "Our dog's really taken a liking to you. But I think Stormy's jealous."

"You two dogs have to be friends." Lynn scolded the animals as they snapped briefly at each other.

Mark helped John Hillman to carry water from the stream. By the time they had prepared and eaten dinner and had tidied up, everyone was ready to turn in.

The caravan was on the road again in the chill, rosy dawn. Lynn and Tim, bundled into heavy sweaters, voiced glum disappointment because they'd had no bear visitors during the night. The highway began to turn sharply west, and soon it climbed to a scene of primitive beauty. "Look, a lake!" Lynn announced. Mark searched on Mr. Hillman's map to find this sparkling blue body of water. "It's called Summit Lake." Mark got a good camera shot to add to his collection.

During the afternoon, they saw Mr. Towers' house trailer parked off the road up ahead. "I wonder why Dan's stopping," Mr. Hillman said, steering his station

wagon well over to the road shoulder. The rest of the
caravan also pulled in and parked.

"Toad River!" Dan Towers grinned and waved at
them all. He pointed to the vivid green water, which
threaded its way along. "Tonight, we'll eat grayling for
dinner."

Time out for fishing! All the men and boys eagerly
got their rods and lines. How glad they were that they'd
taken the time to obtain fishing licenses. Mr. Towers,
remembering that Toad River swarmed with fish, had
obtained bait back at the camper's station.

The fishermen scattered out along the big granite
rocks, while the women and small tots watched from
the riverbanks. Everyone was lucky. Mark made a good
showing. Despite the fact that Tim knocked his father's
can of bait into the river, John Hillman succeeded in
catching the biggest one, about 18 inches long. All the
fish were packed away to be used for the evening meal.

The caravan soon passed by placid, mint-green
Muncho Lake and later over the big steel bridge that
spanned the Liard River. Farther on, they got out to
look in wonder at steaming hot springs that bubbled
up from some seething underground furnace. "Those
springs never freeze," Dan Towers told them. "Even at
sixty below."

The plant growth around the springs looked tropical,
with its lush foliage.

"This seems to be our day for stopping." Mr. Towers'
eyes twinkled at the children. "How about a swim?"

"Swim?" they echoed. "In *there?*"

"Come on. I'll show you."

Sure enough, a foot trail led to an overflow from

the springs that formed a shallow pool. Tim Hillman lost no time in testing it with his hand. "It's warm, just right."

1693946

"Yes, it's comfortable as any heated pool," Dan agreed. "This is fine for the little ones. There's a deeper pool farther on for adults. How are you at swimming, Mark?"

"Pretty fair." Mark was glad that he didn't have to stay with Lynn and Tim and the other small children, as they took turns changing clothes in the Towers' trailer. Soon, the little ones were splashing around with their mothers. As Mark swam in the deep pool with the men, the warm water felt good to his travel-tired muscles.

The fishing and swimming slowed the caravan down, and they did not reach the village of Watson Lake that night as planned. They stopped by Coal River, whose black water, Mr. Towers said, was heavy with lignite. A short side road brought them to the public campground. Nearby, they viewed a lovely spot on the Liard River called Whirlpool Canyon, where the water was tossed, white and foaming, against several rocky islands.

Mrs. Hillman was momentarily provoked with Tim when it was discovered that he'd lost his jacket somewhere along the way.

The homesteaders decided to have a community dinner with the catch of grayling, cooking the meal over one big campfire and all eating together. The men cleaned and fried the fish while the women busied themselves with other foods.

Mark's nose tingled with the appetizing smells. Oh, he was hungry. Would the call for dinner never come?

There it was, at long last. But what was that fuss in
camp? "Bad dog!" Mrs. Towers cried. "What am I going
to do with you?" Mark saw the dessert-loving Pandowdy
slinking guiltily away, with fresh gingerbread crumbs
still clinging to his whiskers. When the hubbub about
the rascally dog had died away, everyone gathered
around for dinner. Mounds of fluffy biscuits were lifted
from reflector ovens. Pans of canned beans were brought
from the fire, bubbling with molasses and brown sugar.
The crisp, golden fish were set out. Then big baked
apples appeared, glossy with crystal syrup and stuffed
with dark spicy mincemeat. "Boy, was that ever good!"
Mark finally pushed his plate away.

The homesteaders lingered around the campfire, talking of many things. Another pot of coffee was put on,
and a big can of macaroon cookies was passed around.

"I know what the children can have," Mrs. Hillman
said, on a sudden thought. "Melted marshmallow treats."
She gave each child several plump marshmallows to
toast over the embers. Then they squeezed the hot
sweet morsels between graham crackers, with squares of
chocolate bars that melted and blended in deliciously.

Mr. Towers started off a round of old familiar songs,
and everyone joined merrily in the singing.

What a perfect day it had been, Mark reflected later,
as he snuggled down in his sleeping bag to get out
of the crisp night air.

Morning found the travelers on the road again, trying
to make up for lost time. An erratic wind stirred tree
branches. Dark, sullen clouds swelled and spread across
the ash-colored sky.

"I wish we could hear a weather forecast," John

Hillman said, switching the car radio dial around. "Reception's poor in the mountains." Mark's transistor radio could not pick up anything either.

On they went, around bends, up slopes and down grades. In an open spot, they stopped briefly for lunch. They got out to stretch, and Mrs. Hillman passed around hard-boiled eggs and sandwiches of canned ham. She poured out canned orange juice, which Lynn immediately spilled all over herself.

"Look, it's clearing." Mr. Hillman pointed to slits of blue in the gray sky, as his wife helped Lynn to change some of her clothes in the car. In the next moment, they heard a distant rumble of thunder. All afternoon, the weather alternated between spurts of brightness and gloom.

Late in the day, Dan Towers' pickup truck developed engine trouble. He pulled off the road at a turnout. Two homesteaders who were good mechanics examined the ailing motor. The caravan had brought along tools and some spare parts for such an emergency as this.

After a short consultation, it was decided that the rest of the caravan should go on while the truck was being repaired. The mechanics' wives would drive their own vehicles. "It's getting late," Dan said. "Find a place for the night and set up camp. We'll be along as soon as possible."

Within a few miles, the homesteaders found a clear spot. "I'd rather not go down into that gully," John Hillman decided, watching one car and a camper slowly descend into a low, bowl-shaped depression. He parked at road level in the meadow with the three other families.

They all had finished dinner, keeping some of the

meal hot for their missing members, when the Towers'
house trailer and repaired truck arrived. Dan rubbed
his chin as he looked at the two vehicles in the hollow.
"I'd feel better if we were all up here. That's a bad
spot if it should rain."

"Look at that clear sky, Dan. It's not going to rain,"
the car owner cheerfully predicted. "It's nice and
sheltered down there, and we're all settled for the night.
The kids are already asleep."

Soon, all the tired company had trickled off to bed.
Mark slept outside as usual, with Mr. and Mrs. Hillman.
They made Lynn sleep in the small tent in case of
sprinkles, and John Hillman put a tarpaulin up over
them all. Tim and Donna were snug in the station wagon.

Mark was awakened in the darkness by sporadic cold
needles of rain jabbing at his face. He burrowed down
into his bag, to no avail. Sleep had been routed by
coldness and rain-laden wind, by sloshing sounds,
voices, lanterns. He struggled up.

Mr. Hillman, in boots and raincoat, touched his arm.
"Come on, Mark, get into the front seat of the car."

Mark quickly gathered up his gear and obeyed. He
discovered that Lynn and some other children had been
taken into the Towers' house trailer. Also, to his surprise,
he learned that it was not the middle of the night, but
six o'clock.

Mrs. Hillman sat huddled in the car while Tim and
Donna slept blissfully on.

"I'd like to help the men," Mark told her. He was
used to wet weather. "I have rainwear I can put on."

"All right, Mark." She peered out into the dimness.
"The storm started all of a sudden. Now the rain is

really coming down! I hope it won't delay us too long."

The rain descended in sheets, streaming down the car windows in a steady flow. Mark found some of the men digging trenches to release water from the hollow down below, which had become a muddy pond. Their hastily dug ditches were no match for the downpour and the heavy runoff, which emptied swiftly into the bowl from all sides. The owners of the car and camper were trying, with little success, to move their vehicles.

Mark got a shovel and began to dig. He glimpsed a streak of lightning. Then thunder crashed all around, its echoes reverberating among the granite cliffs. The men worked doggedly as lightning flashed and thunder rolled. A strong wind swayed the trees and sent rain scudding before it. Mark's wet hands and face felt chilled, while his body perspired. His breath came from his throat in torn gasps. Oh, they didn't seem to be getting anywhere! The two vehicles in the gully were almost hubcap deep in brown water.

Still the men dug. After a while, the thunder began to move southward, each clap growing fainter as it went. The rain seemed to be lessening, too. Mark paused and squinted at the sky. Yes, it was letting up. The worst of the storm was over. Gradually the rain decreased to a drizzle. The backed-up water in the tiny valley began to flow into the trenches and down the mountainside.

Women and children appeared in the gray half-light to view the drenched scene around them. The rain had stopped. "Get back here out of that mud!" mothers shouted, as the children, shrill and exuberant, began to venture forth.

The families were anxious to get going. They could eat breakfast later. The men gazed with apprehension at the surface of the gulch. Patches of slick, pressed-down grass showed here and there in the soft, sticky mud.

When the motors of the two vehicles were started again, Mark held his breath. The camper moved forward only a few feet, the auto not at all. It was just as the homesteaders had feared. Round and round spun the back wheels, with nothing solid to grip.

"They can't get up that slippery incline." Dan Towers' voice was thick with worry. "Without traction, we'll never be able to tow them out of that hole."

4

JOURNEY'S END

Mark slushed through puddles, helping the men to gather from among their belongings boards, sacks and strips of metal meshwork, which they'd planned to use later, in snow. They placed these beneath the wheels of the stalled camper. The driver stepped on the gas pedal. No luck. Slimy mud oozed through the sacks. The boards sank lower and lower. After several unsuccessful attempts, Dan suggested, "Let's try tree branches." The men chopped off a number of bushy, dripping evergreen boughs. Mark carried an armful and placed them on the miry ground under the vehicle. The men used more, then more, since they had them in abundance. The camper tried to inch forward.

"I think it's going to work!" John Hillman exclaimed.

Slowly, the vehicle moved up the incline. Ah, now it was slipping back! "Let's get those boards again." A couple of men pulled the pieces of lumber out of the mud. A new layer of thick boughs was laid, topped by the boards. Another try. Everyone watched intently. Slowly, up, up — this time the straining camper made it over the hump. The corralled children gave a loud cheer. Stormy and Pandowdy joined in the excitement by barking clamorously.

The men used the same procedure with the car that was stuck. After several attempts, they succeeded in facing it up the slope. Then a car was backed to the incline's edge. Two men attached a towline from it to the stranded auto. Other men, hampered by sliding and slipping, spread out the branches, then laid down the boards. When the car below finally got traction, its helpmate drove slowly forward, pulling it up to level ground.

"Glad *that's* over!" John Hillman expressed everyone's relief as he wiped his muddy hands with a rag. They would all clean up at the first facilities they reached.

As though it were a good omen, a shaft of light broke through the leaden skies, giving promise to the dismal day. Soon, the moving caravan was strung out along the northbound road. Their objective for the day was the town of Whitehorse. The morning wore on, and by noon a pale, lemon-colored sun had emerged. The wet green forests exuded a heavy resinous smell.

Dan Towers had told everyone to watch for the bridge at Contact Creek. "There's a sign at the bridge telling how the United States Army engineers working from the south finally met those from the north in October, 1942."

The Hillmans' passengers kept alert as they sped along. "There it is!" Mark saw the sign first.

On they traveled, crossing into the Yukon Territory. "We have to set our watches back," Mrs. Hillman reminded her husband and Mark. As the hours passed, little Donna grew fussy. She was tired of being confined to the station wagon. Tim and Lynn bickered in shrill voices. "Move over!" "Sit still!"

"Here, here!" called Mrs. Hillman. "Look at these pictures. Aren't they strange and interesting?" She produced a travel pamphlet about totem poles.

"What funny old faces," Lynn said without enthusiasm.

Tim frowned at the pictures. "What are they?"

"Years ago in southeastern Alaska and western British Columbia," his mother explained, "several Indian tribes had the custom of making totems, from 10 to 80 feet high. The Haida Indians are considered the most outstanding carvers. They had access to the best cedar trees."

Mark looked through the booklet. "Totem poles sure are hideous things."

"No, Mark," John Hillman disagreed. "They have a deep meaning. The coast Indians had no written language, so the totem was their way of keeping records. Some were symbols of family life or of the power of a chief or memorials of the dead or even house pillars with the owner's crest. There were other types, too."

"I don't see why they had to make them so ugly." Mark's opinion of the totem poles remained unchanged.

"Aren't we ever going to get to the north?" Tim complained, wriggling about in his seat.

Mark picked up the map. "We *are* in the north, Tim. 'Way up in the Yukon. Look." He attempted to interest the small boy, showing him where the long Alaska Panhandle reached down like a pointing finger to St. Rupert. "Right now we're farther north than Juneau, the capital of Alaska."

They passed a big yellow grader and waved to the two men in it. It was one of many pieces of road machinery they'd seen, keeping the highway in good condition.

The scenery began to change as they approached a region of long, fiordlike lakes, whose many bays reached into timbered highlands. They crossed a long steel span over one of these lake "arms," and again Mark took some pictures.

"Look. The caravan's stopping," Mrs. Hillman said. "Where are we now?"

Mark's finger moved along the map. "Near Teslin. The guidebook says that it was a pioneer Indian village."

Mr. Hillman leaned out of the window for a moment. "One of the cars has a flat tire. Let's all get out and stretch our legs."

Everyone in the caravan seemed glad of the chance to stop for a while. The day was clear and bright, and they all breathed deeply of the sharp, bracing air. Several of the men helped jack up the car and put on the spare tire. "He'll get the other one patched first chance he gets," John Hillman said, returning to his station wagon.

Mrs. Towers pointed to the two dogs playing spiritedly with Tim and Lynn. "At last Stormy and Pandowdy are getting used to each other."

When the tire had been changed, the travelers climbed back into their vehicles and pushed onward. Swirls of dust made driving slow and unpleasant for a long stretch. At nightfall, the caravan wearily pulled into Whitehorse, which was located in a valley rimmed by forested hills. It was a treat to have dinner in a neat, shiny restaurant.

How attractive the nicely set table looked. With great enjoyment, the tired, hungry travelers ate the meal that was set before them.

"Whitehorse was a big gold rush town in the old days," Mr. Towers stated over the dessert of juicy apple pie. "Today it's an important travel center."

"Too bad we haven't time to stay over and take one of those Yukon River boat excursions," Mrs. Hillman said.

The homesteaders who owned the campers and house trailer slept in their vehicles as usual. The other families spent the night in a motor hotel. Before Mark dropped off to sleep in his comfortable bed, a happy little thought danced around in his mind. Tomorrow, if they made good time, they would enter the state of Alaska. After that, it would not be long before he and Lynn would be with their father.

Next morning, he found that this feeling of excitement had gripped the whole caravan. They took to the road again, passing the ruins of some old log buildings that Mr. Hillman said the gold seekers had built. Gradually, the trees changed from pines to white and black spruce, and Mark recognized birch, aspen and cottonwood among the dusky green of the spruce forests. As they passed Haines Junction, they saw a ridge of snow-capped peaks in the distance, and later on they drove for miles beside big, blue Kluane Lake. Time went by, and at last the caravan reached the international boundary between Canada and Alaska. The cars all stopped for clearance, and once more wristwatches had to be reset for Alaska Standard Time.

"Alaska! Yay!" The car horns honked and the children

sang and shouted as they drove along the paved highway inside the forty-ninth state. "Alaska is kind of a funny name," Lynn remarked, when they had quieted down.

"Do any of you know what it means?" Mr. Hillman asked. "Some of the first Alaskans, the Aleuts, called it *'Al-ay-ek-sha,'* which means *the great land.*"

He'd have to remember all these things to tell Chuck Wilson when he got back, Mark reflected. For a moment, a little wave of homesickness washed through him. His mind went back to Otsego Falls and to gentle, loving Grandma. He shook off the feeling of sadness. He would always remember his grandmother, but he must now turn his mind to the future. After their Alaskan vacation, he and Lynn and Dad would go home to Otsego Falls together. That night, he could hardly get to sleep. Tomorrow. Tomorrow was the day.

Mr. Hillman didn't have to awaken him. Bright and early, Mark was up, anxious to be on the road. On they traveled, mile after mile on the last lap of their journey.

At noon, the caravan pulled into the junction town of Big Delta for their last quick stop. "Mile 1422" read the sign. This was the end of the Alaska Highway. Mark looked back at the long road as they turned into the Richardson Highway for the remaining 98 miles into Fairbanks. That's where he and Lynn would part company with the Hillmans, who were going on to the Crescent Valley, a curve-shaped lowland to the south. Mark felt that he would never forget the homesteaders and this trip.

Excitement rippled through him when at last the dusty caravan reached its destination, the busy city of Fairbanks. Passersby paused to look in a friendly way at this fresh batch of newcomers in their dust-caked vehicles.

"Look at the log cabins standing near those high modern buildings," Mark said.

"I've heard that this city combines Alaska's past and future," John Hillman remarked. "We'll see lots of contrast up here — the old and the new."

The caravan came to a stop at last. They were here. Suddenly, Mark saw a tall figure get out of an army jeep nearby and stride toward them. "Dad! Dad!"

Lynn heard Mark's glad cry, and all three of them met at a run. "Mark! Lynn!" Their father hugged them hard. "I figured out that the caravan probably would arrive today. I've been waiting since early this morning."

Mark buried his face for a brief moment against the uniformed shoulder. Oh, this was worth coming a long way for. He pulled back and looked up at his father. "Dad, are you okay now? I mean, after the appendicitis operation?"

"Coming along fine," his father assured him. "Still have to take it easy for a while. The doctor won't let me drive yet, so Bill is the chauffeur today." The husky, smiling young serviceman walked over to meet Mark and Lynn.

"This is my father." Proudly, Mark introduced the Hillmans to his father, who shook their hands and thanked them for bringing his children on the long journey from Washington. Then George Bennett presented them with a box he had in the jeep. The Hillmans, opening it, exclaimed in delight as they shook out four parkas, two big, two small, with fur-lined hoods.

"And this is Mr. and Mrs. Towers." Dad met more of the homesteaders. "And here's Stormy. Remember?"

"Stormy!" Dad ruffled the dog's neck hair affectionately. "He was only a puppy when I last saw him."

All the members of the caravan crowded around. "Lieutenant Bennett, you're stationed at Fort Wainwright?"

George Bennett nodded. "I'll be there about a month longer."

Mark helped Bill to load their belongings into the jeep.

"We'll keep in touch with you!" the Hillmans promised.

"'Bye, 'tormy!" Little Donna waved furiously from the station wagon. "'Bye, 'tormy boy, 'bye, 'tormy girl!"

"Good luck in the Crescent Valley!" the Bennetts shouted to the Hillmans. "Good luck to all of you!" they called to the others as the jeep drove away. They headed out of Fairbanks toward the army post. Stormy sat in front beside Bill, his ears alertly turned up. Happiness flooded through Mark, and the weariness of the long trip seemed to melt away. He and his father had so much to talk about — home, their plans. The Hart house — he must tell Dad it was empty, all set for them to move in. How great it would be to have his father home again. Dad, close to the doings at Madison School and seeing Mark pitch for the Otsego Otters.

"Daddy, when can I see some polar bears?" Lynn looked around breathlessly, as though she expected a pair of the big white animals to appear on the road at any moment.

Over her head, Mark and Dad smiled at each other.

"I've never seen one, honey. They live far from here, mostly on ice packs on the Arctic and Bering seacoasts. Alaska has other bears, too — black ones and grizzlies and great big brown fellows called kodiak bears." He turned to Mark. "What do you think of Alaska, Mark, all you've seen of it so far?"

"It's greener than I expected. And it sure looks big."

"Yes, it's green in summer, and it's big, all right." His father nodded. "It's full of untapped riches, too. Besides fisheries, furs, timber, minerals, farms, Alaska is wealthy in oil, hydroelectric power, gas — many resources. All it needs is more people, like those homesteaders."

Mark noticed the intensity of the tone, and he looked questioningly at his father.

"The surprise I wrote to you about," Dad went on in a rush of words. "Guess what? It's a farm I claimed here, in a beautiful sheltered valley. Wait till you see the place. You'll love it as much as I do. Now that Grandma's gone, there's nothing for us in Otsego Falls. But there's a whole new life for us here. We'll get in on the growth of this wonderful state."

What was this — about a farm? About living here? Mark's mind tried to grasp his father's meaning. Not going back home! A chill, like a cold finger, suddenly touched the boy's heart.

5

MIDNIGHT SUN

For a moment, Mark could not speak. Staying in this strange northland to live? He had never dreamed Dad would do that. What about their familiar hometown, the close friends, Madison School? As though from far away, he heard Lynn's excited chatter. "Oh, boy, a farm! Will we have horses, Daddy?"

"No, sweetheart. A tractor."

How could his sister forget Otsego Falls so quickly? Mark stared at Lynn, sitting there contentedly holding Sally Sue. She would be happy anywhere, he thought angrily, as long as she had that rag doll with her. He saw his father glance expectantly at him. *He's waiting for me to say something,* Mark thought. His mouth felt dry, and a lump blocked his throat. All the plans he'd made, all those things he'd wanted to say — he could never say them now. "I — I thought this trip was just a vacation," he managed to mumble, "and that we'd go home afterward."

A shadow crossed his father's face. "I should have written to you about the farm instead of keeping it a surprise." Dad's eyes were troubled. "I guess it was a shock to spring it on you like this. But the claim hadn't gone through the land management office yet. Nothing was settled. Mark," Dad's voice held a pleading note, "you'll like it here. You'll make friends and find that there are a great many outdoor activities to enjoy. It's a different sort of life, but a good one. I was raised on a farm, you know. Bad times came, and we lost it. I've lived in cities ever since. It's something I've dreamed about, Mark — land of my own."

The boy stared at the low, blue hills beyond the city of Fairbanks. "But why 'way up here in the middle of nowhere?" he burst out. "There are farms in Washington, aren't there?"

His father sighed as he looked at him. "Of course there are, but I couldn't afford to buy one there. I'll explain it to you, Mark. In Alaska, a person can make a homestead claim on land to be cultivated up to 160 acres in area. Our claim is in the Rekova Valley." He pronounced it *Ree ko' vah,* and his voice warmed with enthusiasm. "I've been up there to mark our boundaries and start work on our house. The climate is somewhat similar to that of Montana. Wait until you both see the valley. It's sheltered by mountains, with the Wolverine River flowing through. Such scenery! The house is only a small cabin," he admitted with a smile, "and very little of the land is cleared yet. But time and hard work will take care of that. I'm going to work part-time in the valley sawmill to earn money for farm equipment and well drilling."

Lynn shot a volley of rapid questions at her father about the farm and about Rekova Valley. But Mark's disappointment was so bitter that he huddled behind a wall of silence all the way to the family's quarters at Fort Wainwright. So this was how it had turned out, the long-awaited reunion with his father. All the fatigue of the arduous trip seemed to press down upon Mark like a weight.

In the days that followed — queer, long days when darkness never came — Dad took Mark and Lynn sight-seeing on his time off. "We'll start with the University of Alaska Museum," he proposed. "It has a fine collection of Eskimo and Indian artifacts and natural history exhibits."

As Lynn trotted along, she clutched souvenir replicas her father had bought her of forget-me-nots, the state flower, and of a willow ptarmigan, the official bird. In the museum, she admired the weavings and the objects of carved ivory and soft leather. But Mark only stared numbly at them. His mind was far away on Chuck Wilson, his buddy. Would he ever see Chuck again?

"Guess what?" Dad said one morning. "Today, a friend of mine, Greg, who's a pilot, is going to take the two of you on a flight around the area."

Lynn squealed with pleasure, and Mark, too, felt a stir of excitement. But Dad was only doing this to try and win him over, Mark reminded himself when they were winging through the clear blue air with Greg. They glided first over the flat plain on which Fairbanks stood, and Greg showed them big bombers of the Strategic Air Command at Eielson Air Force Base. Farther north, they flew over a chain of milky-green lakes that looked like a frosty jade bracelet.

"Why are the lakes that funny whitish color?" Lynn asked.

"You know what glaciers are — big mountains of ice. Well, they grind very slowly but steadily against rocks beneath them," Greg explained. "They make fine powder that mixes with the water. You'll see lots of that milky water up north."

Sixty miles from Fairbanks, they skimmed above the town of Nenana, and Greg told them that there was great excitement there each spring on the day of the ice breakup in the Tanana River. "Everyone tries to guess the exact day, hour and second the ice crack-up will start. People come from all over to see it. I watched it last spring. The silent, frozen river suddenly gave a deep rumble. Then the ice started breaking into jagged blocks that tossed and crashed."

Mark looked down. It was hard to imagine the smooth, brownish Tanana River beneath them as a noisy, churning mass of broken ice cakes.

Coming back to Fairbanks, Mark asked, "What's that?" and pointed to rippled mounds of yellow mud near a big creek bed. The yellow earth stood out in the green landscape like a swath of crumpled cloth.

"You've heard of the sourdough miner's pan and sluice box?" Greg asked.

Mark nodded. "That was how they washed out gold in the old days."

"Well, this is what has replaced it." Greg waved toward the heavy, throbbing machinery below them. "That's a placer gold dredge. It can work as much as 15,000 tons of earth a day." They saw the machine claw up a huge scoop of gravel. "See?" Greg pointed out. "It's washing and screening that earth for gold." As the machine moved on, it left crinkled yellow mud behind it, like a wide pleated sash.

A few days later, Dad took Mark and Lynn to a baseball game between an army nine and a local team. "I know baseball is your favorite sport," he said to Mark. "I wish you could have been here a few weeks ago for the midnight baseball game. Imagine, no lights needed at twelve o'clock at night."

"The midnight sun!" Lynn clapped her hands. "I like the midnight sun, Daddy."

"I know why." Her father smiled at her eager face. "Because you get to stay up late every night now. But wait till winter comes, with daylight from about ten until two, with an hour of twilight on either side. Then the children go to school and come home in the dusk. I've seen street lights burning here in midafternoon and watched mailmen using flashlights on their routes." Dad turned to Mark again. "In spring and summer, there's lots of baseball in Alaska, both day and night games. Nearly every town has a team."

Mark knew that his father was trying to gain his interest, but the subject of baseball only made Mark more homesick than ever. What were Chuck and the rest of the gang doing? Who would pitch for the Otsego Otters now?

"Here's a letter from the Hillmans," Dad announced one day in the middle of July. "They're going to operate a dairy farm in the Crescent Valley. They've started building their house." Mr. and Mrs. Towers and the rest of the homesteaders had settled in other promising regions, the letter said. One family had gone south to start a blue fox farm. Well, that was fine as long as it was what they all wanted, Mark thought. But he vowed that no one was going to make an Alaskan farmer of him. When he was older, he would earn enough money, somehow, to get back to his hometown. This place was all right for a visit. The long summer days with their evening sunshine, the rugged mountains and deep valleys, the surging rivers, were things to admire and then leave behind. All the sight-seeing in the world was not going to convince Mark that he should live in this upside-down land.

Sometimes, Mark and Lynn went shopping on their own in Fairbanks. One day, Mark found Lynn's chatter unbearable as she babbled on and on. "Look, will you shut up for about five minutes?" he demanded.

"What a big crab you are!" Lynn retorted. "I don't like you anymore. Since we came here, all you do is gripe, gripe, gripe."

Mark bit back the sharp words that came to his lips. It was true. He looked at Lynn, marching along in front of him, her head held high. Mark knew that his sour outlook stemmed from recent resentment against his father. But was it fair to take it out on Lynn? He had a sudden thought. "This way, Lynn. Come on."

With a half-suspicious look, she followed him into a store. Mark was sure this was the place where he had seen them. He looked all around. Yes, there they were. Mark pointed to a pair of tiny moccasins, trimmed with beads. "Do you think they'd fit Sally Sue?"

Lynn nodded, pressing her fist to her mouth in surprise

and delight. She reverently took the little package as Mark paid for it. "Gosh, thanks, Mark." Her blue eyes shone up at him. "I'm sorry I called you a crab."

"Forget it," Mark said gruffly. "Let's hurry up, or we'll never get through."

The day finally came when Dad was out of the army. All the sight-seeing around Fairbanks was over, and they said good-bye to Greg and Bill and all their friends at the post.

George Bennett, now well and strong again, had bought a rattling old red pickup truck to take his family to the remote Rekova Valley. Mark sat, silent and miserable, as the truck, laden with their supplies, bumped along past a wilderness of forests and meadows. He had dreamed of their returning to Otsego Falls in a swift silver plane. What a joke. Every rough jog of the truck made Mark's bitterness more intense.

For some distance, the dusty road followed the winding Honak River. Slow, creaking sounds drifted up from the river, and they saw big 20-foot wooden wheels turning lazily in the water. "Those are native fish wheels," Dad said. "See the two wire baskets on that one? The wheel moves with the current and scoops up salmon and whitefish, which spill down a trough and into a big box. It's customary to let hungry boat travelers help themselves at any fish wheel. See the sheds on shore? The fish are split open and hung there to dry."

Lynn strained to look, but Mark only glanced with bored eyes at a scow tied up at the riverbank farther on. A small tent stood in a clearing, and three husky dogs, chained to trees, leaped and yelped at Stormy, who barked from the back of the truck.

"That's an Indian fish camp," Dad said. "Some Indians live at fish camps all summer. Then when autumn comes they load everything into boats and travel by river to winter cabins, where they trap furs in the woods. In May, before the salmon begin to run, they return with their winter fur catch, which they exchange with traders for supplies."

It sounded like something out of a history book of a hundred years ago, Mark thought disconsolately. What a wild place this was.

"That's a cache," Dad said in reply to Lynn's question, as she pointed to a small log hut on stilts. "Probably belongs to a trapper. It keeps food and supplies safe from marauding animals."

As they jogged for hours over the narrow roads, Mark wearily agreed with his father that Alaska was certainly in need of some good highways. "But air transportation, not roads, is the lifeline of the state," Dad said. "The average Alaskan uses airplanes almost forty-five times more than any other American, and many have their own planes. Bush pilots carry every kind of merchandise you can imagine, as well as passengers. Sometimes empty seats are folded out of the way to make room for mining equipment, or a sled, or a stove somebody ordered. Those pilots are skillful at landing. They can even safely bring down a plane on a river sandbar. You know what pontoon planes are — they land on lakes and waterways. Well, in winter the wheels are changed to skis so that they can land on the snow."

Mark's fancy was caught for a while by thoughts of the useful, adventuresome life of the bush pilot. But after a time, he grew restless again. How far away was this Rekova Valley? He felt as though they were riding to the end of the earth. Whatever had made Dad claim a farm up here, anyway?

"What's that red stuff?" Lynn asked. "It's so pretty."

They had come to the crest of a hill, and miles of magenta-colored fields flamed all below them. "It's a plant called fireweed," Dad replied, "so named because it spreads unbelievably fast during the summer. And those are wild poppies and purple iris in that field."

On they drove, the truck making poor time on the rutted road. Mark felt tired to the bone. He wished they'd get there soon. The comfort of their house would be a welcome change from this jerking vehicle.

Late in the afternoon, they rounded a curve, and Dad said cheerfully, "Well, at last. Here's the village of Rekova. We have to get a few more supplies here."

The village of Rekova. Mark took a deep breath as the truck chugged to a stop. What a huddled little weather-beaten place. They got out, and he slowly followed his father and Lynn into the general store. It was Rekova's only store, selling a bit of everything — groceries, hardware, dry goods — and it had a cubbyhole of a post office in one corner. Mark wandered aimlessly outside as his father and sister chatted with the elderly couple who ran the store.

What a town. He gazed dismally at the cluster of houses nestled against the hillside. Down the road stood a small gasoline station and auto repair shop. A low, square building, the most modern-looking one in sight, was set in a cleared field. Mark walked closer. A sign proclaimed that it was the district high school. The open space was no doubt the athletic field. Mark thought of the junior high school in Otsego Falls, where he had planned to go next year, with its three-story brick building, its landscaped campus, its swimming pool and grassy football field.

"Come on, Mark!" Lynn called. He walked back to the truck and climbed in.

"You didn't even help Daddy load on the things he bought," Lynn said reproachfully.

"Oh." Mark pulled back his thoughts. "I didn't — notice —"

"It's all right, they weren't heavy," Dad said as he started the motor. He backed the pickup away from the store and swung it around. The few people by the building waved good-bye to them. "Well, that's our nearest town," Dad said. "Small but friendly."

Mark felt sick at heart as they drove along Birch Road, which was the main road in this area. Their nearest town — what a place. No movie, no big stores. No soda fountain, or record shop, or any of the things that had been a part of his life. And even this tiny town had been left far behind before they reached their destination.

6

HOMESTEAD IN THE VALLEY

"This is it," George Bennett proudly announced. They came around a sharp turn on Birch Road, and the Rekova Valley stretched out before them. It lay like a deep green cup between slopes of spruce, white birch and aspen. In the strange late sunlight, the Wolverine River gleamed like a wide golden ribbon.

"You'll see a lot of interesting wildlife around here," he told his children. "See that swampy lake? I saw a moose with her calf there last time." He pointed to an oblong of water thick with bright lilies. "It's a haven for all kinds of birds and ducks, too. Some birds go south in autumn, others migrate to Arctic nesting grounds. Look, edible wild fruits grow here. Those over there are raspberries and low-bush cranberries."

Ferns, big and lacy, grew profusely, and rich green moss covered parts of the ground like a velvet carpet. Deep-pink wild roses climbed around tree trunks above the foliage of creeping dogwood. A number of small, silty glacial streams emptied into the big Wolverine. The valley was indeed beautiful, Mark grudgingly ad-

mitted to himself, but so lonely! Were there really houses
hidden here and there among those trees? Dad had said
that when he'd been here before he'd met a family
named Lewis. But neighbors must be miles and miles
apart up here.

"That's where Eldon Lewis and his wife live," Dad
said as a large, attractive log house suddenly came
into view from behind the trees. It had a wide stone
chimney and windows that sparkled in the sunlight,
and it was surrounded by a garden filled with gaily
colored flowers. "They're an older couple who have lived
in Alaska a long time and have made good with their
farm. Their son is a young doctor at Setnek. He serves
all this area, making his visits by plane hops."

"What a pretty house!" Lynn said in admiration. "Is
ours like that, Daddy?"

"I'm afraid not, honey." Dad turned to smile at her.
"Maybe when we've been as successful as the Lewises,
we'll have as big a place. The Rekova store man told
me they're off on a hunting trip now; otherwise we'd
stop in for a few minutes."

As the truck joggled in and out of the road ruts,
Dad pointed off to one side. "There's the grade school."

Mark's mouth set in a hard line as he stared at the
building, which was a good deal smaller than Madison
School, but more modern than he had expected.

"And there," his father waved toward the river, "is
the sawmill. I wrote to them about a job, and they'll
take me part-time."

Mark could see the outline of a small mill farther
upriver. Then they turned from Birch into Eagle Road,
a small, bumpier side road. After a short distance, Dad

steered the truck in and stopped before a log gate. "Guess whose property this is?"

"Our farm!" Lynn excitedly climbed out past Mark and flung the gate open for them. Mark looked around. Dad had been right when he'd said that not much of their land was cleared — only a space around the house. The rest couldn't have been much wilder. They drove slowly down the two ruts that were their driveway, and as they came close to the cabin Mark's heart gave a throb of dismay. So that was to be their new home, that moss-chinked little log hut.

"It has a garden on the roof!" Lynn exclaimed, gazing in rapture at the grassy sod roof dotted with small wild flowers. But Mark looked at the meager windows, the rough door. With a numb, dead feeling, he helped his father to bring their luggage and supplies inside. The house had only two rooms. One had rough bunks in it. The larger room contained a fireplace and stove, a board sink, plank table, some chairs and benches. In a lean-to shed next to this kitchen stood stacks of firewood. A homemade ladder led to a loft. "That will be your room, Mark," his father said. "You'll at least have some privacy."

Mark nodded shortly. Was he supposed to say "Thanks" for — an attic?

"I have lots of work to do on the house before winter sets in," Dad said cheerfully. Stormy and Lynn raced about in the tall grass outside, which was sprinkled with varicolored wild flowers. But Mark stood in the center of the rude kitchen, his mind on the empty Hart house in Otsego Falls, so roomy, so comfortable.

"What do you think of the place, Mark?" Dad asked,

unpacking a crate of dishes and cooking utensils.

Mark's hands clenched into fists by his sides. Well, as long as his father had asked him, why not tell him the truth? "It's worse than I expected," he said bleakly. "And to think —" he whirled around, facing his father, "we could be living in a nice house back home, instead of — this." He jerked his head at the small room.

Dad put down the kettle he was holding. "I'd like to remind you of something, Mark." His voice was low and quiet. "There weren't always houses in Otsego Falls. People had to come over the wild Oregon Trail to build them. There have to be pioneers."

"But why us?" Mark shot out.

"Why not us? Don't you think we've got what it takes?"

"I just don't see the sense of making life hard for yourself," Mark said doggedly.

"Son, you'll find that worthwhile things are seldom easy to come by." Dad put his hand on Mark's rigid shoulder. "Mark, farming is a good life. But don't think that I'm going to force it on you. Have you ever thought what you'd like to be when you're grown — a doctor, teacher, pilot? Alaska's schools are excellent, even in outlying districts. They'll prepare you well for college someday. You saw the fine university near Fairbanks, remember? It's up to you to be whatever you want." The man stepped over to the open doorway and looked out at the land. "Farming is what I want, Mark, and this is the place for me to do it. The farmer can count on about 120 outdoor working days a year here. The growing season is short, but long hours of summer sunlight offset it. Some days have as many as 19 hours of daylight. Besides maturing the crops, that gives the farmer longer working hours."

Lynn jumped from one foot to the other on the tiny porch as she listened. "Daddy, what are we going to raise on our farm?"

"Grain grows well here — wheat, barley, oats, rye. Potatoes and many other vegetables, too. This is good, well-drained soil, although it needs to be fertilized. On the slopes, it is what we call silt loam. Rainfall is adequate, and winter winds are light." Dad glanced over his shoulder at Mark. "Our problem is getting the produce to market. If we owned a small launch, we could bring our farm products right down the Wolverine. Or maybe someday storage and freezing plants will be built nearby."

Mark knew that his father's words were directed at him rather than at Lynn, but he could think of no reply.

"The famous Matanuska Valley once looked as wild as this," Dad went on. "Now they can raise 40-pound cabbages and giant strawberries, among other things. Through the Farmer's Cooperative Association they have electricity, television, telephones. Maybe our future holds all those things, too."

Future! Mark thought angrily. They could have all those things right now, back home.

"Mark," his father's tone was gentle, "I know you miss your friends, especially Chuck. But you'll make new ones. And maybe next year Chuck could fly up here and spend the summer with us."

Next summer. It seemed as far off as the next century. "Sure." Mark turned away.

"This is one very necessary item up here." Out of the corner of his eye, Mark saw that his father was tapping the small radio he'd unpacked. "We have to listen to weather reports, especially in winter. A quick change of weather can be very important. The Weather Bureau here has every scientific device known, and they broadcast the reports regularly. Radio is used extensively for communications, too, Mark. It's called the 'White Alice' network system. It uses ultrahigh frequency radio relays to transmit messages between remote villages and towns. This system is used because it would be too hard to build and maintain wire circuits for telephones across such distances and in extreme weather conditions."

Although Mark merely nodded, he was secretly interested in this unusual communications system and wondered what kind of antennas were used and how the signals were sent out. But he could not bring himself to ask his father any questions and began busying himself by unpacking his own clothes.

After dinner, Lynn followed her father to the shed, where Stormy was being settled for the night. Mark could hear his father's voice. "Look at this little extra room. We have a natural permafrost freezer. It's a cavern dug down into the frozen earth. That subsoil never thaws. We can store salmon, caribou, all sorts of game without spoiling."

As Dad and Lynn went on talking, Mark stirred restlessly. What did he care about crops and climate and how to freeze moose meat? Even the subject of college that Dad had brought up seemed years away. Abruptly, without calling out "Good night," Mark climbed the little ladder to the loft. He threw his jacket on the bunk and hunched over beside the small window. It framed a scene of majestic beauty, but as Mark stared out he pounded his fist against the sill, over and over, in a hopeless way.

On their third day in the valley, George Bennett said to his children, "Let's check some of our boundary markers this afternoon. How about it? We're required to have one in each corner of our claim."

After lunch, the three of them and Stormy set off in the sunshine to see that the markers Dad had placed on the rectangular piece of land were still undisturbed. The first one was a length of pipe set in the ground a short distance from the cabin. They climbed a slope to find the second marker, a sturdy wooden post, also safely in place. Mark gazed down upon their land, seeing the whole claim for the first time. Bennett land. Something that belonged to them. The little brown space around the cabin stood out against the green foliage. But someday more and more of that good earth would be cleared. Mark breathed the crisp, buoyant air deeply. For a moment, he knew how Dad felt about the farm — he could understand his father's hopes. Would these wild fields really produce acres of rich golden grain some future harvesttime? Through Dad's determination and labor, the miracle could well take place. As Mark followed his father along the slope, he was aware that his shirt, like Dad's, was wet with perspiration from the climb. Yet Mark did not feel tired.

"There's a good view from here," Dad pointed out. "See, there's the school."

Mark squinted against the sun as he looked at the

structure, small in the distance. School. Mark's mouth tightened and his mood changed. He did not want to even think about going to school in the Rekova Valley. Memories of Chuck Wilson and the Otsego Otters were still too fresh in his mind. Suddenly, the sun seemed to glare with harsh brightness, and Mark's shoulders curved in a weary slump.

The next morning at breakfast, George Bennett proposed a change of routine. "You've both worked hard getting settled. How about some time off?"

Mark brightened a little. They were to do something different. What was it?

"There's a big blueberry patch beyond that thicket, across the road from our gate," Dad went on. "Would you like to fill a couple of pails while I start clearing the slope? I'll leave Stormy as a watchdog for the house."

Mark shrugged and stifled a sigh, but Lynn agreed with enthusiasm. "We can have blueberry pancakes for breakfast tomorrow!"

"Don't go near the river," their father warned as they set out. "These Alaskan rivers look smooth and calm, with no white, splashing water. But they're deep and powerful."

Mark mumbled "OK." Picking berries — big deal! He trudged out to the log gate as Lynn, in blue jeans and a red sweater, skipped ahead of him, swinging the two buckets. Somehow, his sister's good humor irritated him. She seemed to think that all this sort of thing was great — a novelty, fun. "Wait!" Mark called. Their land faced dusty Eagle Road. A truck, laden with big logs, bumped by. The plaid-shirted driver waved and smiled at them.

"Is that what Daddy will be doing, driving one of the sawmill's trucks?" Lynn asked her brother as she waved back.

"I don't know." Mark glanced without interest at the truck as it turned off near the mill. They crossed the road and entered the thicket on the other side. Soon, they came to the berry patch. Mark began aimlessly plucking at the bushes, his mind far away. What was the gang back home doing now? Something exciting, he would bet. Something that was fun.

Lynn soon had her bucket half full, and she talked endlessly as she worked. "Oh, Mark, it'll be fun when we go to school! I hope I'll meet some girls my age. M-mm." She popped another handful of blueberries into her mouth. "Don't you just love these little berries? Gosh, my hands are black! Is my face black, too? And my mouth? I bet my teeth are all black. Is my tongue black? A-aah —" she stuck her tongue out.

Mark's head spun from her chatter. "Look," he said impatiently, "there's a big berry bush over there, by that stunted tree. Go pick it, and don't talk so much. And quit eating those things, or you'll be sick."

Lynn plunged eagerly through the undergrowth in the direction Mark had told her, the blond braids bobbing like a pair of dancing puppets.

Mark's mind returned to thoughts of home. He could see Chuck Wilson's house again, right next door. Not like this lonesome place, without a neighbor for miles. He and Chuck used to talk to each other from their bedroom windows. They had even rigged up a rope pulley to send items back and forth, a book, a baseball glove, a candy bar.

Mark sank down on the sun-dappled ground and began to draw lines in the dirt with a stick. The lines formed a baseball diamond. Vaguely, Mark heard Lynn moving in the distance, but his mind was filled with the memory of his schoolmates' cheers as he struck out one opponent after another in league games. Mark Bennett, star pitcher of the team.

What chance would he have to use his baseball skill now? What chance to do anything? He broke the stick he was holding with a quick hard snap. On and on he sat, immersed in deep gloom.

At last, Mark got up heavily and looked around. He couldn't see Lynn. He called to her. There was no answer, and he called again. Alarm prickled through him, and he rushed in the direction she had taken. "Lynn! Lynn!" Where could she have gone?

The woods stretched out around him, somber and secret. Surely she wouldn't go in there — she might get lost! Mark threshed back again through the bushes, calling frantically. He came out of the thicket to where the swift river flowed. Then he saw it on the steep riverbank — Lynn's bucket, lying on its side, the berries spilled and scattered.

7

NEW SCHOOL

"Lynn!" Mark yelled her name over and over in panic. He ran along the bank, staring at the ponderous, topaz-colored river as it surged along. No! She wouldn't go near the edge. Dad had warned them. But — he looked in anguish at her bucket.

Mark turned and ran to the road, tripping over roots that swelled out of the ground like knotted veins. His heart pounded with beats of dread, and his breath came fast and ragged. Oh, why hadn't he watched Lynn, watched her closely? She was unaware of danger, not used to the open spaces of the country. He threw back the gate and ran down the lane. Dad — he must get Dad. Where was he? Mark tried to remember. The slope. Dad had said he was going to work on the slope.

Panting as though his heart would burst, Mark stumbled on toward the cabin. A bit of blue flashed among the greenery. It was Dad's denim work shirt. Then he saw his father digging the ground near the house. "D-Dad!" Mark had no breath left.

His father looked up. He dropped the spade and ran to Mark.

"Lynn —" the boy gasped.

Dad seized him by the shoulders in a tight grip. "Lynn's here, Mark!" Dad looked into Mark's face. "We were going to find you as soon as she got cleaned up."

Safe — was Lynn really safe? Mark's shoulders heaved as he stared dazedly at his father. "She's all right." Dad gave him a little shake.

Suddenly, the cabin door flew open. Lynn — that *was* Lynn, wasn't it? — popped out, blueberry-stained from head to toe. Her face was a purplish blur beneath the flaxen hair. Mark sagged like an empty sack. As his eyes focused on his sister, he felt the strange urge to laugh and cry at the same time.

"You've had a bad fright, Mark." His father's voice was gentle. "But everything's all right." Mark could feel Dad giving his shoulders a final squeeze.

Lynn trotted over to her brother. "I — I guess I should've found you and told you I was going home." She gave him a timid, black-toothed smile.

Little sisters! Mark wanted to grab her and shake her till those blueberried teeth rattled. But instead he pulled her to him in a quick rough hug. "I should've watched you, you — little pill." he mumbled, pushing her away again.

Their father nodded. "But she shouldn't have run off, either." He looked sternly at Lynn. "Don't do anything like this again."

"I heard a motorboat on the river, and I just went to see it," Lynn explained with wide eyes. "I walked all along the riverbank watching it. The man waved to

me, too. But then I couldn't find the blueberry patch
again." She lowered her tone dramatically and leaned
toward Mark. "Something moved behind me in the
bushes. I think it was a bear!"

"More likely a marmot," was her father's opinion.

"I got scared." Lynn's eyes looked enormous in her
purply face. "I ran and ran and finally came to the
road. So I made it home from there. The bear," she
concluded with a sigh of relief, "didn't catch me."

Bear! Mark scoffed in his mind. But something really
could have happened to her, he thought with a shiver.

"I cleared all the underbrush I could from that slope
today," Dad said. "I'll get on with it another time."

Mark, still feeling drained and shaken from his scare,
followed his father and sister to the house, where Stormy
lay dozing on the porch.

"We both lost our buckets of berries," Lynn mourned.
"Now we can't have blueberry pancakes for breakfast
tomorrow."

"You've eaten enough of them for a while," her father
declared. "I think you've got as much on the outside
of you as the inside. Come indoors and get washed."

"Hello, there!" a deep voice called out. They turned
on the porch to see a big man with sandy-colored hair
striding down their lane. He wore work clothes and a
pair of heavy brown boots. "Heard there was a new
family in the valley," he said in a cheerful, booming
voice. "I was on the river and waved to the little girl
a while ago. My name is Harry Bates. I have a farm
a few miles up the road."

He was probably their nearest neighbor, Mark thought.

"I'm George Bennett. Glad to know you, Harry." Dad

stepped forward and shook hands. "This is my son, Mark, and Miss Blueberry here is Lynn."

The man patted Lynn's head. "Say, when you pick berries it looks like you mean business!" He turned to Mark. "I have a boy about your age and two smaller boys. They're visiting their uncle in the Panhandle now. You'll meet them when school opens." Then Mr. Bates began talking to George Bennett about climate and farm conditions. Stormy sniffed around the stranger with interest, finally seeming to accept him and subsiding back to his comfortable spot on the porch. Mark followed Lynn into the house, where she began trying, without much success, to remove the berry tints from her skin and teeth. The doll, Sally Sue, propped up in a chair, seemed to gaze at her little mistress with benign eyes. Mr. Bates' strong voice could still be heard in snatches of conversation. ". . . used to live down on the Panhandle . . . glad to see more people here . . . lots of good land still unclaimed . . ."

"I wish Mr. Bates had some girls," Lynn said as she wiped her face halfheartedly. "You're lucky to get a boy your age for a pal."

Lucky! Mark thought wryly. He had no wish to meet this unknown farm boy. What would they have in common? He looked curiously at his sister. "Lynn, do you really like it here?"

The little girl paused, holding the soapy washcloth in her hand. "I — I don't know. I miss Kathy and Susan and all those kids. But don't you think it's kind of fun, Mark? Sort of like camping."

Fun? Mark snorted impatiently. "Camping is only fun for a while."

"Well, anyway," Lynn began to rub her chin again, "it's nice to be with Daddy."

Mark felt a warm flush spread over his face, and it angered him that he should feel ashamed. Why should he feel guilty about not wanting to stay here? No normal boy would prefer this place to Otsego Falls. Lynn was only a little girl, easily satisfied. She didn't feel things deeply. But when you were older, it was different.

Through the small window, he saw Harry Bates bid good-bye to Dad and go off down the lane. "Nice fellow," Dad said as he came in. "He does his traveling by boat. Sometime, we might need his motorboat and he might need to use the truck. People up here help each other and share things. In winter," Dad's eyes twinkled as he looked at Lynn, "we might even have to borrow somebody's dog team and sled."

"Daddy, really?" Lynn asked in an awed tone.

"Really. Harry Bates said that sometimes the roads can't be cleared fast, and people get snowed in."

Lynn grinned, her teeth looking like a row of raisins. "Oh, boy, what fun!"

"Not exactly fun," her father said with a smile, "but it could certainly be interesting."

The days marched relentlessly by. Signs of autumn appeared in the golden carpets of leaves shed by the birches and in the flocks of geese and waterfowl winging southward. And for the first time Mark saw another sign of approaching winter, the dramatic flashing of the luminous northern lights.

"Look! First they were yellow; now they're all colors!" Lynn cried breathlessly as they watched. "Daddy, what makes the sky light up like that?"

"There are several theories. One is that the lights are

caused by electrical discharges in oxygen and nitrogen, with the sun as the source of energy." Dad looked quizzically at Lynn. "You don't understand? Well," he patted her arm, "there's another version. Some people believe that the aurora borealis glows through the magic of Aurora, goddess of the dawn."

"Aw, that's only a legend," Lynn scoffed. But from the way her eyes shone, it seemed that she liked the second explanation better.

Mark could not help but be moved by the radiant, irridescent spectacle, too. How truly beautiful the northern lights were as they swung lightly from one horizon to another in a graceful, shining arc. In many ways, the north was a strange, wonderful land, unlike any other place on earth.

One day, the Lewises, the neighbors in the big house, paid the Bennetts a visit, inviting them over for Sunday dinner.

On Sunday morning, Mark was awakened by rain slashing against his window. He looked out at the valley, blurred and indistinct behind its wet gray curtain. Then, he smelled the tantalizing aroma of bacon. Quickly, Mark got dressed and went downstairs, to find his father cooking bacon and scrambled eggs. Food was expensive in Alaska, but George Bennett believed that nourishing meals were important for health and strength. It was warm and cozy in the cabin as they lingered over breakfast. Lynn toasted bread on a long-handled fork held near the stove's heat, and they spread the crisp slices with blueberry jam.

In midafternoon they drove to the Lewises' in the pickup truck. It felt good to dash out of the rain into the big room with its glowing log fire. Eldon Lewis' home, with its tastefully furnished rooms, was spacious and comfortable. They were one of the families in the area who had a two-way radio. Mrs. Lewis was not only jolly and kindhearted but also a marvelous cook. After dinner, she wrapped up large portions of food for the Bennetts to take home, including a great many of the delicious little spice cakes with which Mark couldn't help stuffing himself.

The Lewises' great pride was their son, the young doctor, who had chosen to stay and work at his profession in this state where medical care was sorely needed.

*　　*　　*

All at once, the short Alaskan summer was gone, and autumn had arrived. It was time for the fall school term to begin. Mark looked toward school with a touch of dread. He was bored in the quiet valley, yet he had no enthusiasm for this new experience. When the unwelcome opening day came, he followed his father to the truck with dragging footsteps. George Bennett would drive them to school only the first day. After that, Mark and Lynn would take the bus, which passed their gate at eight o'clock each morning. School was already in session when Dad parked the pickup truck outside the yard. Mark saw that the school building was even newer than he'd thought.

As they opened the classroom door, a score of faces turned to look at the newcomers. The teacher put down her book. She was a small woman with soft, dark hair. As she came forward to meet them, she reminded Mark a little of Chuck Wilson's mother, back home.

"Good morning." Her voice was low and pleasing.

"I'm Miss Elliott. Welcome to Valley School."

George Bennett spoke with her for a few moments about his son and daughter, and then he left. Lynn looked around with great interest, but Mark gazed stonily at the ceiling. He disliked being one of the targets for all those eyes. He dropped his gaze to the rows of faces. *Well, what're you looking at?* he felt like asking.

"Boys and girls," the teacher's pleasant voice addressed her class, "here are Mark and Lynn Bennett, who are new in the valley. Let's try to make them feel at home."

She led Lynn to the next classroom. Through the open door, Mark could see a plump, older woman greeting his sister. Lynn was then seated behind a golden-skinned girl with short straight hair and bangs like black satin, who smiled shyly at her.

Miss Elliott returned and directed Mark to a seat between two big boys. "This is Ralph Bates." She introduced a husky, sandy-haired boy of about fourteen. So this was one of Harry Bates' sons. "His family's farm is over your way, Mark."

Mark gave a brief nod. In this wild, spread-out state "over your way" could be any distance from 10 to 50 miles.

"And this is Tom Anahuk," Miss Elliott went on, "who lives a bit farther upriver." The Eskimo boy's black eyes crinkled into a smile.

Mark sat down, and the teacher gave him some textbooks and workbooks and explained briefly about their use. Then she went back to conducting a lesson for one small group, while the other pupils did written work she had assigned them. Mark looked around the unfamiliar classroom. Wide windows with a sweeping view took up the side walls; a blackboard stretched across the back. Rolled-down maps hung on each side of the teacher's desk.

As the pupils' attention drifted away from him, Mark began to observe them. Their ages ranged from about ten to fourteen. Nearly half the students were Indian and Eskimo children. They had the same type of haircuts and wore the same style of clothes as the others. Mark was to learn that everyone's shirts, jeans and cotton-print dresses came from a mail-order store in the faraway town of Setnek. Some of the children wore jackets that seemed to be popular with people in the north, soft leather, possibly caribou, trimmed with colorful native designs.

Mark counted the heads, light and dark, that were bent over their work. Only twenty-two students. Probably about the same number in Lynn's room. There had been over five hundred at Madison. Ralph Bates and — what was his name? — Tom Something, were the only two boys close to his age. What in the world could he have in common with them? Mark thought of Chuck, and a surge of loneliness swept over him. This strange school, this whole big raw land was just unbearable. If only he could get away from here.

The time dragged on, punctuated by a short recess. Would noon hour never come? It did, at last, and the pupils clattered to outdoor benches to eat their lunches. Mark started to follow Ralph and Tom, then changed his mind and ate his sandwiches alone. He was anxious to get to his dessert, the last of his favorite fudge that Mrs. Wilson had sent. Idly, he watched a small Eskimo boy with a limp hobble after a ball nearby. I bet he's never tasted homemade fudge, Mark thought unexpectedly. On a sudden impulse, he called the boy over and gave him all the candy, brushing aside the boy's surprised thanks.

After a while, the two big boys, in blue jeans and plaid shirts, ambled over to Mark. "New here, huh? Where'd you come from?" the one named Ralph asked.

"Otsego Falls, Washington."

"I never heard of it. Is it a big town?"

Mark crumpled his paper bag. "Big *city.*"

Ralph's eyes looked Mark up and down, taking in the gray pants, the blue sport shirt. "You're the first *cheechako* we had around here in a long time."

Mark's face flushed. He knew that it was a Chinook Indian word meaning a newcomer to Alaska, a tenderfoot. He'd heard people in Fairbanks refer goodnaturedly to the homesteaders as *cheechakos.* But he didn't like this country boy's tone.

"Where'd *you* come from?" Mark countered. "Or have you been up here in the woods all your life?"

Ah, I got to him, Mark thought with satisfaction as the smile faded from Ralph's face. Mark could see the boy's fists clenching. Was Ralph going to strike him? *Go ahead, hit me,* Mark gritted silently through his teeth. He'd teach this farmer to make fun of him.

But the Eskimo boy stepped forward between them and spoke quickly. "Ralph's been here a couple of years." His dark eyes bored into Mark's face. "I'm the one who's lived here all my life."

The bell rang, its strident sound cutting through the noontime noise. Tom Anahuk turned away, and Ralph followed him. Mark let out his breath and began walking after them. So they were against him, right from the start. Probably jealous of his clothes and of the things he'd seen and done in a big, interesting city. Well, Mark didn't want their friendship anyway. He saw Lynn laughing as she finished up a game with Ruth, the Indian girl. Lynn was too young to miss her old friends.

Mark joined the pupils shuffling into the schoolhouse. As he passed Miss Elliott on the steps, holding the bell, he felt her gray eyes upon him in a long, measuring look. Had she seen the incident in the yard? Mark shrugged. She seemed nice enough, and he had no wish to make trouble for her. Still, he was not going to let these valley boys push him around.

After school, all the students except the Bennetts were soon whisked away in the bus. Mark and Lynn had been told to wait this first day for their father, who would pick them up on his way back from an errand in Rekova.

Mrs. Schultz, Lynn's teacher, stopped at Miss Elliott's room before she left. "Lynn, tomorrow after school some girls are coming over to my house. I have a piano and they like to sing and learn about music. Will you come?"

Lynn agreed with enthusiasm. "I'm sure Daddy will let me."

"Mrs. Schultz's husband is in the Forestry Service and is often away from home," Miss Elliott told the Bennetts. "She enjoys the children's company."

The teacher gave the willing Lynn a job cleaning chalk trays and erasers. Then she asked Mark to help her stack books in the shelves of a room down the hall.

"This is our little library. We're trying to add to it. Valley School has a promising future. As you see, only two classrooms are in use now. But as the Rekova population grows we'll be ready for it with this fine new building."

"Yes, ma'am." Mark could think of nothing else to say.

Miss Elliott glanced at him. "When you're new in a place, it's hard. I remember how it was when I first came from Michigan."

"Michigan? You're a long way from home."

Miss Elliott looked at him steadily. "This is my home now."

Mark frowned as he handed her the books. "You mean you'd stay here, by choice?"

"I didn't intend to at first," she said. "The man I was going to marry came here as an oil company engineer. He wrote to me about how much he liked Alaska, and so we planned to live here. But he — was killed in an accident at his work. Later, I came to see Alaska as he had described it. Only for a visit, I thought. I liked it, and there was a need for teachers; so I stayed." Miss Elliott's eyes looked beyond Mark to the green mountains outside the schoolhouse window. "It is a great thing to be needed, Mark. Before coming to this valley, I was in a more remote part of the state, where I helped in all sorts of emergencies. I've given first aid, served as a ham radio operator." She turned and looked earnestly at him. "It really is true. People who help to build a new frontier always receive more than they give."

Mark moved away. He might have known that the conversation would turn into a sermon. Miss Elliott followed him and pressed two books into his hands. "Read these, Mark. They may help you to understand this big state."

He glanced at them — histories of Alaska.

"You'll find that this is a melting pot of nationalities,"

the teacher went on. "Eskimos and Indians were here first. It's believed that they came from Asia centuries ago across Bering Strait. Early in the eighteenth century, the Russians came and later Yankee whalers and missionaries. The big gold rush in 1898 brought nearly every race in the world to Alaska's shores."

Mark grudgingly took the books as his father's pickup stopped outside and Lynn called to him. He had no intention of reading them. In a week or so, he'd bring them back.

But without television or other once-familiar diversions for his spare time, Mark found himself reading the books and being surprisingly interested in them in spite of himself. Okay, he admitted silently at week's end, so Alaska had a colorful history. And it was true that its scenery was spectacular, its climate unusual. That still didn't mean that a boy like Mark would be happy here.

"How's school?" George Bennett asked more than once.

Always Lynn would blithely voice her approval, while Mark would mumble "All right," and escape before further questions might be asked.

Someday, Mark wrote to Chuck Wilson, *I'm going to come home. I miss the school, the team, your family, everything I had to leave behind. I don't know yet how I'll get away, but someday I'll work it out somehow.*

Miss Elliott mailed the letter for him, as she often did for valley people. If she only knew what was in it, Mark thought. Miss Elliott, so sweet and agreeable, didn't realize that it would take a lot more than books to change Mark Bennett's mind about Alaska.

8

UNSCHEDULED FLIGHT

On the following Saturday, Mark found that a long, dull afternoon stretched out before him. His father was involved in some extra work at the mill. Lynn and several of her classmates were having lunch with Mrs. Lewis. Lynn had brought Stormy along to show him to her friends. Mark had been invited, too. Were they kidding? Who wanted to be around a crowd of jabbering girls?

He stood on the cabin porch, tapping his foot impatiently as he gazed across the valley. What could a person do in this desolate place? Take a walk, what else? He struck off down the lane. Maybe he'd go over to the sawmill. No. He changed his mind as he crossed Eagle Road. He was not in the mood to have his father see him and introduce him to his fellow workers. "This is my son, Mark," his father would announce, while the men stared at Mark. Then he'd have to make polite conversation with them, answering "Fine," when they asked how he liked Rekova Valley. No, thanks.

He strode toward the Wolverine and walked along

its bank for more than an hour, hitting a stick against trees as he passed. The afternoon was bright and cool. At intervals, a strong breeze blew in from the river. As always, Mark's thoughts returned to Otsego Falls. It seemed a hundred years since he had parted from Chuck Wilson and his other friends. Would he ever see them again?

Mark gazed at a black arc in the clear blue sky. It was a big bird, dipping in graceful circles. A hawk, Mark guessed, hovering over some poor unsuspecting prey. A short distance ahead at a curve in the river, he saw two men fishing from the bank, on the same side of the Wolverine as he was. Mark didn't want to be bothered talking to them. He threw down the stick and turned away from the river, ambling through the trees.

Suddenly, he came to a clearing where a small gray panel truck was parked. The fishermen's, no doubt. Had they caught anything? Mark approached and leisurely examined the front seat. Nothing there. He walked idly around the vehicle and opened the back door. No fish. The men probably had their catch with them in their creels. But — something caught his eye — what was that pile of stuff at one side of the truck? Curiosity nipped at Mark. He entered on his knees. The door swung closed, and he turned around in alarm. He let out a relieved breath to see that the door could be opened from inside. He crept forward. Canvas — it was only a big piece of half-folded canvas, crumpled and paint-stained. He turned part of it over and saw various-sized paint cans with lids and one large can from which brush handles sprouted. Painting supplies, that was all.

Mark started to slide out when he heard voices. Oh, no! The men were coming. Through the small back window he saw that they were almost here. Mark froze. What excuse could he give them for being in their truck? They'd think he was up to something. He bit his lip in exasperation. What a stupid predicament!

Suddenly, hope flickered. Maybe they were just coming to get something from the truck. They'd go away again. Then he could get out. Mark sank down and lay flat. He pulled the drop cloth over himself, making a cone-shaped air passage with one hand. The odor of paint pressed around him.

The men opened the back door. Mark lay motionless, his body taut as strung wire. He heard them mention the towns of Rekova and Setnek. Then Mark felt the rods and other fishing gear being thrust in beside him. Don't cough, he warned himself, as his breath seemed to strangle in his throat. The canvas felt rough and coarse against his face. Would they never get through? At last, the men slammed the door. Mark drew a deep breath. He could smell the fish. Now go, he willed the men, *go* so I can get out of here.

But the men didn't leave. They got into the cab of the truck. In a moment, the motor hummed. Of all the rotten luck! Now what? Through the metal wall between him and the men, Mark could hear them talking. He sat up and his thoughts spun around in a confused whirl. Should he make his presence known, tell them the truth, that he had been harmlessly snooping? Supposing they didn't believe him? They might drag him to his father, accusing him of attempted theft or something. It would be better if he slipped out

and made a dash for it. Now was the time, right now, while the men were absorbed in conversation, while the truck was slowly picking its bumpy way between trees.

Mark drew himself out from beneath the canvas and wriggled toward the double door. But within the next moment, he realized that he'd waited too long. With one last bump, the truck turned sharply to the right and immediately began to pick up speed. It was too late to jump out. They were on the road now, going fast.

Mark's tongue gave a click of irritation at himself for getting into this silly plight. Half-listening to the men's voices, he knew that he had no choice but to disclose his presence. He hoped that they would release him without a lot of humiliating questions. From their talk, he discovered that the driver was going as far as Rekova, and that the other man — called Ted — had left his car there, and then would drive on to Setnek.

I should speak up at once, Mark thought. It would be a long walk back, even now. And every moment was bringing him farther away from the cabin on Eagle Road.

He was about to bang on the front wall of the truck and shout to the men, when like a zinging arrow a quick unbidden thought flashed into his mind. Away from the cabin, away from Rekova Valley, *away* . . .

Mark's call died unspoken, and his heartbeats quickened. He let his arm drop. The impulsive idea spread and grew. It blotted out reason. It overshadowed every other thought. Mark had wanted to get away from the valley. He would have given anything to get away.

Here, through pure chance, was the perfect opportunity. Setnek, then Fairbanks, then — somehow — home to Otsego Falls.

Excitement rippled through Mark as he settled back in the truck. He moved around from time to time to keep his legs from growing stiff and cramped. The odor of fish grew stronger than that of paint, but Mark was too busy pondering his escape to pay much attention to unpleasant smells or personal discomfort.

Transferring, unnoticed, from the panel truck to the other man's car in Rekova was his problem. How could he do it? After feverishly devising and rejecting half a dozen schemes, Mark realized that he'd have to wait and see what happened and then seize any chance he got. If he was caught, well, that would be the end of that. He pushed that thought away. He'd make it. With a little luck, he'd make it.

One thing was in his favor. There seemed to be no reason for the driver to remove the canvas. No doubt it was connected with his job, and this must be his day off.

On sped the truck, mile after mile. The ride seemed interminable to Mark in his nervous state. He hadn't thought the village of Rekova was so far away.

At length, he felt the truck slowing down. Mark scrambled in beneath the canvas. His mouth was dry as dust, and he tensed up into knots. The truck stopped, and the men came around and opened the back door. Mark's heart hammered with such loud, thudding strokes that he felt sure the men would hear them.

The man named Ted seemed to be taking out his fish and gear. As soon as the door banged, Mark threw off the drop cloth. After a moment, he cautiously peered

through the window. His eyes watered from the sudden
exposure to light, even though it was the waning light
of late afternoon. Three cars were parked near Rekova's
small general store. Which one was Ted's? None of
them? The two fishermen walked on past the cars. Their
backs were toward Mark. His gaze swept the scene. As
far as he could see, no one else was around. Perfect!
He slipped out, closing the door silently, loosely. Hiding
behind the truck, he peeked out to observe the two
men. They stopped beside a blue four-door sedan that
stood at the edge of the nearby pine grove. The taller
man — he must be Ted — put some of his things into the
trunk. Then Ted unlocked the front door and rolled
down a window. He left his fishing rod sticking out
of this window as he and his friend walked over to
the store.

Mark's pulse raced. What a lucky break! But he'd
have to hurry. They might only be going to get some
small purchase. He darted in among the trees and slid
along like a shadow. Now the blue car was just a few
yards in front of him.

The sound of voices made him melt back into the
shrubbery. He watched as a man and two small boys
turned in from the road and headed toward the store.
Darn it, anyway! They were walking in this direction.
Mark would appear as though on center stage if he
stepped out into the open. *Hurry,* he silently urged
them. Oh, that dumb kid! Mark pounded one fist against
the other — what was he doing? Bending over to tie his
shoelace. Come on, hurry it up, Mark implored. The boy
uncoiled and ran after the others. There — they were
inside the store at last.

Mark hastened to the blue car. Before he'd quite reached it a man and woman came out of the store, carrying parcels. Had they seen him? He couldn't tell. He tried to keep his actions normal and unsuspicious as he opened a rear door. The couple, occupied with their own business, got into one of the parked cars. The roar of their motor gave Mark the covering noise he needed to slam the car door tight. Then he crouched down on the floor, his heart pounding like a bass drum. There was nothing under which to hide this time. One glance of the man Ted into the back seat and that would be the end of Mark's journey.

He heard the sound of crunching footsteps, then voices of the two men. He hadn't secreted himself a moment too soon! They called out a few parting words. Then the driver moved in behind the wheel. Soon the blue car sped along the road to Setnek.

Mark closed his eyes in sheer relief. So far, so good. After a while, the hump in the middle of the floor made his body ache. Drafts of wind chilled him. But no discomfort could dispel his exhilaration. Oh, the wonderful sense of freedom, the glory of escape.

All at once, a jarring note shoved its way through his mind. For the first time since he'd set out, Mark thought of his father. How worried Dad would be by Mark's disappearance, how upset — making a frenzied search of the valley. Mark tried to stifle the thoughts. He reasoned that in these things someone had to get hurt a little. In time he'd let his father know his whereabouts.

He moved slightly to relieve pressure on his back. It was no improvement. He was afraid to turn around.

Any sound might betray him. On they traveled. Mark's
head began to throb. He felt hollow with hunger. Oh,
he had to change his impossible position, he just had to.
The noise of the engine would drown out the small
rustling sound, wouldn't it? Putting his palms flat on
the floor to support him, he eased himself around. That
was better, for a while, anyway.

A new worry began to gnaw at him. After Setnek,
then what? Could he hitchhike to Fairbanks? His father
might have a general alarm out, complete with Mark's
description. If he got to Fairbanks immediately, could
he stow away on a plane to Seattle? He'd read of
someone doing that in another place. Could he manage
it? And if that weren't possible, how could he cover all
those miles to Otsego Falls? He'd work it out one step
at a time, he thought doggedly. Then Mark thrust
the worrisome thoughts from his mind.

Outside, daylight began to give way to dusk. From
his awkward location, Mark could see the darkening
sky. It flew by in jerky patches framed by the window,
making Mark dizzy, so that at last he closed his eyes.
More miles. More pains and aches. He huddled on the
hard floor, shivering in the path of biting air currents.
If only he'd worn his heavy jacket. If only he'd brought
a lunch with him on his walk. If only he could stretch
or sit up. If, if . . .

Onward they rode, and it seemed to Mark as though
they were hurtling endlessly through space. Twilight
became night. He welcomed the velvet darkness as an
ally, a friend.

At length, Mark felt the car slowing down. Cold
wings fluttered in his stomach. Were they approaching

Setnek? Yes. There were lights, traffic noise, the sounds of a town. Mark drew up his knees and squeezed in against the front seat. Would Ted go straight to his house? Put the car in the garage? Mark hoped so. Then he could slip out.

The car turned sharply, slowed down and stopped. It was not beside a house, Mark could tell that much. This brightly lit place pulsed with sound and motion. Voices, automobiles. And what was that clean, pungent smell? Gasoline. A wave of dismay washed over Mark. They were at a service station. He tried to flatten himself into invisibility.

"Fill her up, Bert," he heard the driver say.

He could hear the pump hose being connected to the tank as the two men spoke about fishing. "Yeh, pretty good luck today." That was Ted's voice. Mark felt open and exposed with all those lights shining in on him. Get it over with fast and get out of here, he soundlessly begged the driver.

Their conversation went on as the attendant lifted the hood and later banged it down. Mark shrank back as Bert passed the window. He heard the hose being removed. Now, they should go.

The men had stopped talking. Still, Ted didn't start the motor. A new sound came to Mark's ears for a moment, a squeaky, sliding sound that was familiar, yet which he couldn't identify. Ah, now he knew. Cloth or paper rubbing against glass. And with the knowledge, his heart sank. Bert was polishing the car windows.

Only do the windshield, only the windshield, Mark hoped in anguish. But in a moment he saw the shadow of the man cleaning the front side window. Mark buried

his face in his two arms on the floor. Without his white
giveaway face maybe he'd appear to be no more than
a bundle of clothes. Mark didn't move, he scarcely
breathed. Was the man doing the rear window now?
Mark strained to hear the polishing strokes. What was
it that he heard instead — a gasp, an exclamation? The
boy's heart became a lump of lead in his chest. He
knew how Bert's face must look — astonished, incred-
ulous. He heard the rush of footsteps around the car,
the excited announcement to Ted, the flurry of move-
ment, the rear door being flung open.

Then Mark was sitting up, blinking in the strong lights,
numb, bone tired, frustrated.

Afterward, Mark would remember with a pang the
rest of that miserable night. Faces would float through
his recollections. Ted, Bert, two state policemen, a cluster
of curious onlookers.

"Running away from home?" Ted still hadn't gotten
over the surprise of unwittingly aiding in the attempted
escape. "Why, kid? Why?" His tone was sympathetic.
"Do your parents beat you or something?"

"Leave him alone. He's worn out," one of the officers
said. "You hungry, boy?"

Mark gulped down a few spoonfuls of hot, thick soup
in the restaurant to which he was taken. But ravenous
as he'd thought he was, he couldn't eat any more. It
stuck in his throat. What would they do with him now?
Put him in jail?

"Rekova Valley." In a low tone, he answered all the
officer's questions. "Two-way radio? Yes, Mr. Lewis has
one."

Soon, they had contacted Eldon Lewis, who in turn would notify George Bennett that his son had been found in Setnek.

"Nothing more to do." The officer looked at Mark in a kindly way. "Better get some sleep. It will be morning by the time your father gets here."

In bed at last — not in jail, but in another officer's home — Mark lay rigid and wide-awake. He dreaded facing his father, who probably was on the road now in his pickup truck, weary, agitated and furious.

"Why did you pull such a stunt?" his father would angrily demand. "Of all the senseless things to do!" he might add in derision.

Yes, getting from here to the state of Washington as a runaway was an impossible scheme. If Mark had stopped to think it through, he would have scorned such a plan as being doomed to failure. His only escape was at least four or five years away, when he could earn money for a plane ticket. He squirmed at the thought of his stupidity. When news of this foolish venture got around, Mark would become the laughingstock of the valley.

He finally fell into a troubled sleep, from which he awakened early and unrefreshed, with his nerves jagged.

How awful he looks, was Mark's first thought at sight of his father. A stab of guilt touched him. Had exhaustion and anxiety made his father's face so gray and haggard? Mark's glance fell. He couldn't meet his father's eyes.

George Bennett got the business at hand over with quickly. He didn't humiliate his son in front of anybody. Mark inwardly thanked him for that.

They had driven out of Setnek and were on the road before either one of them spoke. "Have you nothing to say?" his father asked at last in a tight voice.

Mark mumbled an automatic, "I'm sorry." How flat and insincere it sounded. He could see Dad glancing at him.

"Sorry because you caused trouble and worry, or because your escapade didn't succeed?" As Mark remained silent, his father went on, "Is it really so terrible living here with your sister and me? So unbearable that you can't stand it?" He shook his head in a bewildered way. "I don't get you, Mark. I don't understand you at all."

Mark stirred uncomfortably on the seat. He wished that his father would shout at him, ridiculing the whole absurd episode. That would be preferable to seeing this pain and perplexity etched on his father's face. But George Bennett didn't rant and yell. After a while, he didn't even speak. Most of the long trip was covered in silence, as though a heavy oppressive curtain had fallen between the pair of them.

9
CONFLICT

During the next week, Mark tried to ignore Ralph Bates' constant needling. How foolish Mark had been to betray the fact that the harmless name, *cheechako*, annoyed him. And now Ralph had more pinpoints for his tormenting jabs — the knowledge of Mark's ill-fated ride to Setnek. Mark had hoped that perhaps only Mr. and Mrs. Lewis knew of the incident. But of course everyone knew, since his father had driven all around the valley looking for him. At school, Tom Anahuk said nothing to Mark, but occasionally the new boy caught those dark eyes upon him in a contemplative gaze.

Lynn mixed in happily with the other children. Sometimes, she brought her doll Sally Sue to share with her special friend Ruth.

One crisp afternoon, the Bennetts got off the school bus as usual at their farm gate. Mark was surprised when Ralph Bates and Tom Anahuk got off, too, because their stops were farther on. Lynn ran down the bumpy road to the cabin and was soon out of sight. Stormy barked to greet her, and then the dog ran on to meet Mark.

Tom suddenly spoke to Mark. "Do you want to see a boat I'm building at the river bend?" He pointed to a spot downstream from the sawmill.

Mark looked suspiciously from Tom to Ralph. Why this sudden friendliness? They must be up to some trick. "I can't. I have to help my father." He turned away with Stormy.

"Even his dog is a *cheechako*." Ralph laughed. "Ilik would fix his dog, huh, Tom?"

Mark angrily whirled around. "Stormy's a good dog! Loyal, smart."

"Not smarter than my dog." Tom's eyes glinted.

"Bet he is!"

"Come on. We'll see."

"Okay!" Mark agreed. "I'll show you." Stormy trotted along trustingly beside Mark as they crossed the road and passed through a grove of white birch. Then Mark saw the half-finished hulk of a small boat on the Wolverine's bank. So Tom's first invitation hadn't been a trick after all. The Eskimo boy really was building a boat.

Suddenly, Mark heard a low growl, like distant thunder. Then he saw a big white dog straining powerfully at a chain attached to a tree. "This is Ilik," said the Eskimo boy. "When I work on the boat he keeps me company. My little brother brings him here before I come from school." Tom stood proudly beside the animal. "Ilik's a Siberian husky I raised from a pup. Someday he'll be lead dog on a team. Maybe he'll even be in the big sled-dog races."

Mark had heard of the strong, intelligent huskies who competed each March in the North American Championship races. He was about to admire Tom's handsome, blue-eyed dog and to admit that of course Ilik was smarter in that respect, since Stormy had never worked on a dog team. But Ralph's quick voice cut in ahead of him. "Try them out!"

Tom looked at the silent Mark with piercing eyes. What was Tom going to do anyway? Then, as though he had waited long enough for Mark to speak, the Eskimo snapped off the chain. The big white dog circled Stormy, who seemed puzzled in his friendly way. Then Ilik rushed in, snarling, and Stormy sprang away. But not fast enough! Mark's heart leaped into his throat as he saw that his dog's flank was slashed. Tom's dog was strong, wild and cunning. He could kill Stormy!

"Stop it!" Mark yelled. "Stop it!"

But Ilik circled again. Although Stormy gamely stood his ground and faced the husky, Mark knew that his dog wouldn't have a chance. He heard Ralph's excited cries blending with the growls of the animals. Suddenly, Mark leaped in between the two dogs. The animals drew back, startled for the moment. Mark seized Tom by the front of his plaid shirt. "Call off your dog!" he cried. "Let's you and I fight it out instead!"

Tom took hold of Mark's fists and jerked them away. "Ilik!" He whistled shrilly, then sprang forward and grabbed his dog's collar as Ilik pulled against him. The boy's slant black eyes glittered at Mark. "The two of us will fight tomorrow."

Ralph pressed in eagerly. "Have it in the woods after school."

"I'll be there," Mark grimly promised. He motioned
for Stormy to follow him, and he walked swiftly away
from the birch grove. Poor Stormy. Mark glanced at
the blood on his dog's coat. He felt sick with guilt as
they went through the gate and down the lane. He
was glad no one was in the house as he washed the
dog's wound and put antiseptic on it. After the bleeding had stopped, he found that the cut was not as deep
as it had seemed. To his relief, Stormy slept peacefully
most of the evening, and neither his father nor sister
noticed the dog's injury.

Since Mark's return from Setnek, tension had settled
over the household like a cold chill. If the worn-out and
distraught George Bennett had said little on the ride
back, he had found plenty to say to his son afterward.

"When you've finished high school you can go
wherever you want. I'll even pay the fare," he told
Mark in a stiff, clipped voice. "Meanwhile, you're never
— understand? — *never* to attempt this running away
again." Mark listened in silence — giving no sign of the
agreement he felt — as his father grimly enumerated the
hazards of getting lost in the forest or swamp and
the futility of reaching faraway Seattle. The one aspect
George Bennett didn't mention was voiced one day by
Lynn, when the brother and sister were alone. "Daddy
was dashing all over like a — a crazy man. We thought
you got drowned or something." The little girl's voice
trembled as she recalled the frightening worry. With
an impatient hand she rubbed away the quick tears.
"You're a rat, Mark Bennett! You used to be nice. But
that's all you are now — a big rat!"

Girls, so tearful and emotional, Mark scoffed as he turned away. Then he remembered his own panic when he'd thought Lynn was lost. And that had been for less than an hour, while his father had worried nearly all night.

Mark was glad every day to get out of the strained atmosphere of the house. But now conflict had come to him at school, too.

When Mark got on the bus next day, excited whispers ran like a ripple of wind through the pupils. Ralph Bates apparently had spread word of the coming fight. Mark could not concentrate on his studies that day. He sneaked nervous looks at Tom Anahuk every chance he got. The Eskimo was not as tall as Mark, but was solid and stocky. He was no doubt strong as a bear from the vigorous life he led, Mark thought gloomily. Well, Mark would just have to do the best he could.

After school, most of the pupils waited at the roadside for the bus. Lynn was among them, and Mark saw her gazing anxiously at him. The dismal thought came to him that his father probably would punish him for getting into a fight like this. A group of boys talking excitedly slipped into the nearby woods and Mark followed them. His heart beat very fast as he saw the eager boys forming a ring around Tom, who stood waiting in a small clearing.

Well — Mark took a deep breath — he might as well get it over with. The circle of boys parted to let Mark through. Tom stood, poised and watchful. Mark lashed out at once, but the blow did not land. Again he struck wildly, while the black-haired boy nimbly danced away.

The yells of the stamping boys pounded against Mark's ears like roaring surf. He paused to catch his breath. In that instant, his opponent's brown fist rocked him.

Mark shook his head to clear it. He'd have to be much more cautious. He stepped around Tom, guarding his face. He saw his chance and landed a blow to Tom's body.

The Eskimo retaliated with a one-two punch. Mark stumbled on the uneven ground, and the spectators roared.

"Look, he's getting knocked out!" Mark heard one of them screech.

Knocked out? I only tripped! Mark strove to regain secure footing. Fury at the onlookers seemed to give him a new spurt of strength. He pounded away at Tom, but the boy was elusive as a lizard, always darting out of reach.

Mark was getting short of breath. Already his legs felt tired. Tom Anahuk looked fresh and alert, as though he could go on for the next hour. He surprised Mark with another strong blow that set loud hammers punching within his head.

Mark tried to circle around Tom, attempting to corner him, to pin him down. Stay still for a minute, Anahuk, stay still! But again Tom sidestepped away. Round and round they went.

Ah, Mark saw an opportunity. He got one in, with all his weight behind it. But Tom moved so that it partly glanced off his jaw. In the next moment, Mark felt a powerful punch on his nose. He knew from the sudden warm gush that it was bleeding. There was no doubt about it. He was getting much the worst of this fight.

Suddenly, over the screams of the boys came a voice of authority. Their yells trickled into silence. Mark looked around dizzily and saw Miss Elliott, whose calm, sweet face was twisted with shock and worry. Quickly, she sent the spectators to catch the bus, and she ordered the two scuffed fighters along the path and into her little blue car. "What would have happened," she asked reproachfully, as she started the motor, "if I had not come to investigate all the yelling?"

Neither boy answered. Mark held a reddened handkerchief to his still-flowing nose. He could feel the pressure of Tom's broad shoulders as they sat squeezed together on the front seat. What a clever, skillful fighter the Eskimo boy was, Mark thought in secret, grudging admiration.

Miss Elliott drove them to the little home on Birch Road where she lived alone. The neat cabin was topped by an emerald green sod roof, dotted with small, bright wild flowers. A log fence hemmed the house in, and the gate was decorated with a big set of bull-moose antlers, an adornment Mark had seen often in the north.

"Come inside," Miss Elliott said. She made Mark sit down. Then she tipped his head back and applied pressure to his upper lip, while holding a cold compress at the back of his neck. "Tom, get a basinful of water and bathe your face," she ordered. He silently obeyed.

Mark's nosebleed stopped at last, and he felt better. While the teacher and Tom cleared away the towels, Mark's eyes wandered about Miss Elliott's house. It was no larger than the Bennetts' cabin, but what a vast

difference there was in beauty and charm. The log walls
and rafters had been smoothed and burnished to a golden
glow. Two bearskin rugs lay before the stone fireplace.
Small carved ivory figurines — a polar bear, walrus, even
a family of tiny ducks — marched along the polished
wooden mantel.

Miss Elliott followed Mark's glance. "Even a simple
log house can be made cozy and pleasant." She smiled
at him, then pointed to the rugs and ornaments. "Gifts,
from the parents of some of my pupils." Her tone became grave as she looked from Mark to Tom. "This is
no way for strangers to get acquainted. Will you boys
shake hands now and be friends?"

Tom changed from one foot to the other and looked
questioningly at Mark. The blond boy cleared his throat,
about to speak. But a rebellious little thought silenced
him. Mark reminded himself that Ralph and Tom had
started the trouble, with that big, vicious dog. His face
hardened, and as he turned away he saw the Eskimo's
expression change, too, the lips tightening into a thin
line.

Miss Elliott sighed and shook her head as the two
boys remained motionless and silent, their hostile eyes
avoiding each other. "Come. I'll drive you both home."

Why didn't she scold them? Mark wondered. Why
did she give no threats or warnings about future fights?
He stole a glance at the teacher and saw that her
attractive face had lines of weariness in it. She was
probably too tired and disgusted to bother anymore
with pupils who made a nuisance of themselves.

Mark tried to keep his shoulders from touching Tom's

when they sat in the car, but it was impossible. He could even feel movements of the Eskimo's breathing as they rode along. How tense Tom's clasped hands looked on his lap. Such strong hands. Mark winced as new aches hammered through his jaw. When the car turned into Eagle Road and pulled up at his gate, Mark jumped speedily out. "Thanks for the ride home and — everything," he said to the teacher, looking past Tom's graven profile. He wanted to add, "I'm sorry," but the words just wouldn't come out. Then the blue car was gone, and it was too late.

Now to face Dad, Mark thought, and his shoulders sagged with tiredness. His body was sore, and his head throbbed. Yesterday, Stormy had come home stained with blood, but no one had known. He looked down at his jacket. Today he was the one, and the evidence was easy to see.

Lynn opened the door. In a voice vibrant with sympathy, she whispered, "I didn't tell Daddy about the fight." She might call him names at times, but there was no one more loyal. Fright filled her eyes when she noticed his jacket.

"Only a nosebleed." Mark kept his tone low.

Lynn tugged at his arm as he passed by. "Did you win?"

Mark could not make himself shake his head. How he hated to admit defeat, even to Lynn. She'd hear about it soon enough at school, he glumly thought.

His father came in from the shed, and Mark saw the same look of quick fear clouding his eyes. "Are you all right?" Dad stepped forward.

"It was only a nosebleed," Mark repeated. He straightened up and looked at his father. "I was in a fight." *Don't ask me who won.*

"I see. Who were you fighting with?"

Mark took off his jacket. "Some wise guy Eskimo." He started to pass by his father, but Dad stood there like a rock. Mark looked up and saw that his father's eyes were like cold blue steel.

"Want to tell me about it?"

Defiance sparked Mark's reply. "We just fought, that's all." Why should he reveal the incident about Stormy now?

"I heard that you thought you were better than anybody else at school." Dad's voice was low and controlled. "I didn't believe it — then."

Mark felt a warm flush staining his face. Who'd been telling his father things about him? He threw Lynn a half-accusing glance. No. Lynn was no tattletale. Miss Elliott, then. "So you and the teacher have been having a heart-to-heart talk about me," Mark said in a surly way.

"Drop that tone." Dad did not raise his voice, but the note of authority was strong in it. Mark stood before him, silent and sullen. "It happens that your teacher and I did talk about you, because we both care what happens to you. Miss Elliott said that you needed understanding and time to adjust. She didn't say one word against you."

"Then who —?" Mark blurted out.

"It doesn't matter," his father said tersely. "The unfortunate thing is that the ugly rumor seems to be true."

He looked evenly at his son. "You'll have to change your attitude, Mark, and try to get along with the people in the valley." His voice softened. "Is there some way I can help you, something I can do for you?"

Mark shook his head.

His father turned away. "Go and wash up for supper."

As Mark washed his hands, he suddenly knew where his father had heard about his actions at school. From the young Bates boys, who'd been with their father when Dad had spoken to Harry Bates yesterday. They'd no doubt picked up the remarks from their loudmouthed big brother Ralph and had repeated them within Dad's hearing.

Now what? Mark wondered, as he gingerly touched his sore face. How was Dad going to punish him? But no punishment seemed to be forthcoming. Maybe he thinks I've been punished enough, Mark grimly guessed, looking into a small mirror at the welts and bruises that Tom Anahuk had inflicted upon him.

"We had another letter from the Hillmans," Lynn chattered at dinner. "The Towersers visited them last month, and Tim said that Pandowdy, the dog, is up to his old tricks. This time it was Mrs. Hillman's berry pie that he ate."

"The Hillmans might drive up and see us soon if they get the chance," Dad said. "Here's their letter." Obviously trying to smooth things over, he passed it across the table to Mark. "Here's one from Greg, too. Remember him, the pilot in Fairbanks? He's going on a visit to Seattle soon."

Lucky Greg, Mark thought, as he silently read the letters.

Mark lay awake for a long time that night, dreading the thought of going to school the next day. Everybody would know what a poor showing he had made in his battle with Tom. Anyway, what *had* happened to Mark in the fight? He was strong and quick on his feet. He'd even had some boxing training at summer camp. Mark had to admit to himself at last that there was only one answer. Good as Mark had thought he was, Tom was better. What would happen if they tangled again? Mark felt worried. Well, all he could do would be to fight the best he could, even though Tom might end up whipping him badly.

Mark found next day to his relief that he had no worry about the Eskimo boy starting anything. Tom Anahuk, silent and proud, avoided Mark with elaborate care, and Mark in turn paid no attention to him. But Ralph Bates was another matter. Ralph and a group of smaller boys, whom he openly encouraged, jeered all day at Mark in low tones. Two of them were Ralph's younger brothers, the little blabbermouths who'd gossiped to George Bennett. Everybody at school knew that Miss Elliott had saved Mark from a real beating, he thought in humiliation, trying to close his ears to the whispered taunts, the hissing names.

After school, Tom got off the bus at Mark's stop, near the bend of the river. Ignoring the others, he headed for the birch grove. He was going to work on his half-finished boat, Mark guessed, with his big white husky for company. Ralph Bates and his crowd of young followers got off. They lingered idly by the roadside until Lynn ran down the farm lane.

As he reached his gate, Mark suddenly felt a heavy

hand upon his shoulder. He spun about and looked up into Ralph's scowling face. The other boys, breathless with anticipation, clustered around.

"All right, *cheechako*," Ralph said softly, "teacher's not here to help you now. So, you think you're too good for us, city boy. Well, I'll show you. I'm going to finish what Tom started."

10
GOOD NEWS

Mark stiffened. Not another beating! He was still sore from the last one. And Ralph Bates was bigger, older, stronger-looking.

Ralph swung without warning, before Mark even had time to think. Mark caught the full shattering impact of it on his jaw. He could hear the small boys shrieking with excitement.

Sudden anger ran through Mark like a warm tide. He threw down his schoolbooks and braced himself. Then he struck a strong blow that connected with Ralph's big body. The boys grew silent as they tensely watched. The only sounds on the clear September air were the thuds of the fighters' fists against flesh, the scufflings of their feet upon the hard-packed ground and grunts of pain and breathlessness. As the punches went swiftly back and forth, Mark realized with surprise that the big sandy-haired boy had neither the speed nor strength of Tom Anahuk. Ralph was slowing down, throwing wild blows, breathing heavily now. Again Mark caught Ralph — and again. Mark would beat him! Victory was like a sweet taste in his mouth. Mark almost had him. One more well-landed punch would do the trick. Mark skipped jubilantly around the big boy, watching for an opening.

Ralph's pale eyes shifted around as he backed away. "Get him!" he called out hoarsely. "Butch, Bobby, all of you — get him!"

The ring of boys closed in on Mark. He struggled desperately, but they came at him in a rush from all sides, hitting him with fists and schoolbooks. At last, Mark fell heavily to the ground.

"That's enough!" Ralph Bates cried, wiping his face with his sleeve. "Somebody might see us. Let's go!" They sped down Eagle Road as a lumber truck approached.

Mark picked himself up and limped painfully to the farmhouse. He was glad to have the place to himself for a while. His father was working at the sawmill for a few days, and he could see Lynn playing up on the hill with the fast-healing Stormy. Mark felt better after he had washed, but the new cuts and bruises were impossible to hide. If only he'd had a fair fight, Mark thought in anger, he would have beaten that big bully. Imagine Ralph, the coward, calling on his little brothers and their friends to help him.

"Did you fight Tom again?" Lynn asked when she came home, her eyes round with surprise at her brother's new blemishes.

"No. Somebody else," Mark answered shortly.

At the end of the day, Dad came in from the sawmill. After one glance at Mark, his face seemed to become tired and drawn. Although he didn't mention Mark's newly battered appearance, his sober look seemed to say, "Fighting again!"

If only Mark could explain that this fight was in self-defense. But as long as Dad chose to ignore the subject, Mark thought with stubbornness, then so would he.

"I bet you won this time," Lynn whispered loyally, as she helped him to bring a load of firewood from the shed.

"For Pete's sake, will you stop pestering me?" Mark snapped. Immediately, he was sorry for his sharp tone. Poor Lynn probably had to defend his name every day at school. It wasn't her fault that her brother couldn't seem to come out ahead in any of these fights. "Let me carry that wood for you," Mark gruffly mumbled.

"Here's the mail," Dad said, taking some letters from his shirt pocket. The mail — a big event up here. Our one link with civilization, Mark thought in scorn.

"It's from Chuck Wilson, and I got one from his mother," Dad said. From Chuck? Mark's interest was instantly caught as his father handed him the letter. He sat down at the table to read it.

"Hope your father will agree to the plan," Chuck had written in part. Plan — what plan? Mark looked up to find Dad's eyes upon him. "I don't know what Chuck means."

His father tapped the other letter from Otsego Falls. "Mrs. Wilson wrote that if it was all right with me, she'd be glad to have you come back and live with them. She said that you and Chuck were almost like brothers." He looked steadily at Mark. "You could continue at Madison School and be with all your old friends again."

Mark's heart skipped a beat. The Wilsons, the good, kind Wilsons, had been touched by Mark's homesick letter. Now they had made this great and wonderful offer. His spirits soared. Back again with Chuck, who really was like a brother. Back at the old school. Back pitching for the Otters once more. But — would his father agree? Mark looked questioningly at him.

"Remember my friend Greg, the commercial pilot?" Dad's tone was heavy, as though with fatigue. "He's going stateside in a few weeks for a visit. You could fly back with him."

Mark nodded, half-afraid to speak. It might seem disloyal to his family, but oh, he wanted to go so much. And who could tell? Dad might give up this farming idea and come back, too. No. Mark knew in his heart that his father would not give up. Dad would try to make a success of this farm with every ounce of skill and strength that he possessed.

His father gravely studied him. "Mark, you seem very unhappy here. I want to do what's best for you. I know you'd have a good home with the Wilsons, and I would pay them for your care. A satisfactory arrangement could be worked out." He paused. "You want to go back, don't you?"

"Oh, yes, yes!" Mark said fervently. Then the look on his father's face made him realize how emphatic the words sounded, as though he couldn't wait to leave. "Everything's so different here," Mark added lamely.

"Most Alaskans are transplanted people," his father pointed out. "You didn't give it a fair chance. But this will be your own decision." Dad got up, and Mark thought for the first time that his father looked sort of old. "I'm disappointed, of course, at the way things are turning out. But I'll never hold your decision against you, Mark. If you leave, I'll understand. And we'll always keep in touch."

So, just like that, it was settled. Mark could go home. As soon as his father contacted Greg and the departure date was fixed, Mark would write the good news to Chuck. Home! Mark lay awake late that night in his attic loft, thinking of the wonderful things that were in store for him back in Otsego Falls.

The next morning when he got on the school bus, Mark felt a surge of satisfaction when he saw Ralph Bates. Ralph's face was dominated by a black eye. The eye was swollen closed, its blue-black bruise extending from cheek to temple. Well! Mark had made at least one punch count. Then he shrugged with indifference and turned away. What did he care about this country boy now?

After a while, he noticed Tom Anahuk's glance going from Mark's newly nicked face to Ralph's purplish eye. "What happened?" Tom finally asked Ralph.

The big boy looked sheepish. "I — I finished your fight."

Tom jumped up like a shot. "I don't need anybody to fight for me!" His gaze flashed around the bus. "Who saw the fight?"

The small boys cringed down in their seats.

"Who saw it?" Tom's words were like whiplashes.

"Ralph yelled for us to help him," Butch admitted in a mumble.

"The *cheechako* was winning the fight," Bobby Bates whined.

Tom whirled on Ralph, and all the schoolchildren held their breath. "You fought him, too!" Ralph cried, shrinking back.

"In a fair fight." Tom's voice was like ice. "Listen, all of you." His arm swept past the boys' faces so fast that their eyes blinked. "This *cheechako* fought me to save his dog, which he loves. Which of you would spare your dog or fight single-handed among strangers?" The Eskimo's voice thickened with contempt. "None of you. The *cheechako* is worth more than all of you put together."

Mark got a glimpse of Lynn's radiantly shining face. He looked in surprise at the angry Eskimo, whose eyes gleamed like burning coals at the cowering farm boys. Then Tom turned to Mark. "I'd like to show you the boat I'm making." Tom's voice was low and steady. "Will you come someday — Mark?"

Mark Bennett started to say "No." He wasn't interested in this boy's boat. But as he looked at the strong brown face, he realized that this was the proud Tom's way of offering friendship. Well, why not? Mark would only be here for a few more weeks anyway. He nodded. "Sure, I'd like to see your boat — Tom."

From then on — now that Mark knew he was going home he decided to make the best of the time he had left in Rekova Valley. His changed attitude was reflected at home in the willing help he now gave his father.

The days were growing shorter, and time seemed all too scarce for the many tasks Dad had to do. Clearing the land was a hard, expensive job. A small section was now free of stumps and growth, giving promise of how fine the whole claim would look some distant day.

"After the second year," Dad told Mark and Lynn, "each homesteader must show proof that he has culti-vated some of his land."

To earn the money they needed, George Bennett worked as often as he could in the nearby sawmill. The mill prepared white spruce for poles and mine timbers, as well as for lumber and fuel. But this job wouldn't last into winter, because the sawmill closed down when the river froze. "I wish we had a caribou or two in our freezer, for the winter," Dad said one day. "I'm going to take time out for a hunting trip soon. Meanwhile, we can catch some fish and small game. How about it, son?"

Mark agreed, and so the following Saturday was set aside for a fishing trip. It worked out well, because Lynn and Ruthie, the Indian girl, were to spend the day at Mrs. Schultz's house.

Early on Saturday morning, Mark and his father sped down the Wolverine in a small motorboat borrowed from Old Ed, at the mill. Spruce and birch lined the banks of the big river, which was still being fed from ice that had begun melting away back in the spring thaw. They passed by a narrow channel, where spiraling wisps of smoke and a big fishing wheel disclosed an Indian fish camp. Huskies barked among the trees as their boat roared by.

Today, Mark was aware of a return of the old, close

feeling he used to have for his father before the arrival
in Fairbanks last June, when news of the farm had
made Mark withdraw into himself. It felt good to be
pals with Dad again, Mark thought contentedly. His
father really had been very fair about letting Mark
return home. In his wildest dreams since coming north,
Mark had never thought his problem would be solved
so generously by his father.

I'll save money all year from my Otsego Falls paper
route, Mark thought, and fly up next summer to visit
Dad and Lynn.

"Ed told me of a good place to try," his father
remarked, steering the boat along in the strong current.
Wind rushed past their faces like the powerful wings
of huge, unseen birds. Overhead, a plane hummed.
Mark squinted up at it. Was it a bush pilot, perhaps
bringing medicine or supplies to some out-of-the-way
village? No, this plane was larger, an Air Force craft
on its way to one of the northernmost military bases.

Mark's glance dropped back to the pulsing Wolverine.
"What kind of fish will we get?"

"Most likely grayling and Dolly Varden trout."

"Where are the big salmon I've heard about?"

"The Katmai region, in western Alaska, for one place,"
Dad replied. "King salmon, 20 to 40 pounds, are a prize
catch."

"How many kinds of salmon are there, anyway?"

"Let's see — dog salmon, the red or sockeye. There's
the silver, or coho — half the size of the king, but a
great fighter. Pink, or humpback. Many kinds."

The boat slid into the tributary that Old Ed had
recommended as a good fishing ground. George Bennett

carefully guided the boat away from low, dragging sweeper branches. The only sign of life was a circling hawk. They stopped in a placid spot. Dad baited his hook and began the patient waiting of the fisherman. In a pleasingly short while, he had landed a Dolly Varden.

Mark was not so lucky. "Try this," his father suggested as Mark baited his hook for another try. "The grayling has a great appetite for flies."

Dad was indeed right. And when Mark had hooked one, he discovered that the grayling also had a fierce instinct to fight. The fish thrashed and pulled up, down and across current. Twice, Mark almost lost it. Then the spirited grayling leaped into the air, and when it found itself still a prisoner, it made a fast run downstream. Mark had never realized how thoroughly a small, wild thing could exhaust its pursuer.

"Good work, Mark!" his father exclaimed when the boy finally landed it. "Say, it's at least 20 inches." Dad's praise gave Mark a happy feeling. "Look, Mark, it's very much like the Dolly, except that the grayling has a big dorsal fin."

The morning passed quickly. By noon, they had made a good catch between them for the permafrost freezer out behind the little cabin. At the end of the day, Lynn came home, happy and excited, from the teacher's house. Mark looked at her in a puzzled way. There was something different about her. Then he knew what it was. Lynn's bright, eager face usually looked out from between two untidy yellow pigtails. But now her smooth, golden hair had been combed and tidied and tied with red ribbons.

Dad noticed, too. "Say, honey, that's the best way your hair has looked since you came to Alaska. I'm afraid neither my attempts nor your own ever turn out very well."

"Mrs. Schultz fixed it for me."

Her father gave her an affectionate little shake. "Looks like Mrs. Schultz will make you the belle of the valley."

Lynn *did* look cuter for having a little attention, Mark thought to himself. It was hard for a girl to grow up with only men in the household, who knew nothing about feminine style.

"What a lot of fish you caught." Lynn didn't care for fish on the menu, although she now tolerated small helpings of certain kinds.

"Don't worry, you won't have to eat them all at one time," Mark assured her. "Besides, we're going after game birds soon. You'll like them better."

The following Saturday, father and son went on a short trip, and again Lynn was occupied with interests of her own. A group of the younger valley children were meeting at the Lewis home, where Mrs. Lewis, at her piano, would supplement Mrs. Schultz's music lessons with other favorite songs.

Mark knew very little about hunting, but Dad was a good shot. He used a small-bore shotgun that required accurate shooting, and Mark couldn't help but admire how his father handled it. Before the day was over, his father had bagged a good supply of ptarmigan and grouse.

"We do what all good hunters do," Dad told Mark, as they returned home, weary and contented, with

the game birds. "We shoot only the amount of game
that we need for food."

What a thrill it would be, Mark thought, to go out
for three or four days after moose and caribou. His
father would need all his hunting skill and luck to bring
down one of those big, wary fellows. It would indeed
be an accomplishment for the Bennetts to come trium-
phantly home, laden with their winter supply of meat.
Then a sudden little thought harshly jarred through
Mark's daydream. He realized with a queer pang that
when this long hunting trip took place, he would be
far away from Alaska.

11
SWIFT RIVER

A few days later, Mark was able to take time out from his chores to go with Tom Anahuk to the bend in the river. He left Stormy at home, not trusting Ilik to be as friendly as his master.

"Come too, Ralph?" Tom invited, but the other boy sullenly refused. Mark knew that Ralph resented the new companionship of the *cheechako* and the Eskimo boy.

The two of them walked through the birch grove to the place where the Wolverine turned in a wide arc. Sometimes, Mark had seen heavy, flat-bottomed boats on the river, but today it was deserted. Off to his left was the berry patch where Lynn's disappearance had given him such a scare. Across the river, big currents eddied around a large spruce tree that had fallen from the steep opposite bank when its roots became undermined. Deeper roots, embedded in the rocky bank, held the fallen spruce there despite the buffeting waters.

"Ha! Good boy!" Tom rumpled his husky's white coat with affectionate fingers, as Ilik greeted him with

frenzied enthusiasm. The dog's inquisitive nose sniffed
Mark, and then apparently satisfied, Ilik turned back to
his master.

Mark gave his attention to Tom's half-finished boat,
as the Eskimo boy explained about his work on it. Tom
tapped the boat skeleton. He described to Mark how he
had sawed the gunwales and ribs of his craft by hand
and then had planed them smooth with great care. "I
measured and figured out everything." Tom pointed to
the bow, then the stern. "My friend Joe, in the mill,
helped me. He shaped these two plywood pieces into
curves."

Mark saw where they were skillfully joined to the
keel with screws and glue. He looked with new interest
and admiration at Tom's painstaking job. "Did Joe
teach you all about building boats?"

Tom shook his head. "Eskimo boys learn about boats
from their fathers. Since the old days, my people made
kayaks from walrus skins. Big umiaks, too." Mark had
heard of the light yet sturdy native craft. The kayak
had especially interested him. His father had told him
that it was a small boat in which one man sat and
propelled the craft with a two-bladed paddle. So small
was the boat's opening and so securely did the Eskimo
attach his parka to it that kayak and passenger could
roll over in the open sea without being swamped.

"Last year," Tom went on, "Fred, my trapper friend,
made a wood and canvas boat like this. I helped him
and learned. A heavy boat is not good for a boy to
handle on the Wolverine. Too hard to fight the strong
current. But this light boat will ride easy as a kayak
over the water."

Mark nodded as he pictured the finished boat in his mind. "Yes, like a canoe."

"When there's no wind, I'll paddle. For wind, I'll put up a sail," Tom planned. "The frame's not lopsided," he remarked with satisfaction. "It would be dangerous to have the boat off-balance."

They began to work together, talking of many things as they sanded the 15-foot by 40-inch frame. Mark was surprised to hear of all the different places where Tom had lived.

"We used to live near the coast," the Eskimo boy related. "I liked it there. But the catch of seal fell off in our village. Some families decided to move inland where there would be more food. We traveled over wild tundra where no trees ever grow. In some places, I saw mosquitoes like black clouds in the swamps. We lived for a while beyond the big river, the Yukon, with lonely hills all around and wolves howling through the still winter nights. It took a long time before we found a place where we really wanted to settle." Tom paused and gazed far off over the mountains. "I liked the sea, stretching away so big and wide."

He misses the sea, Mark realized, looking at his friend's wistful face. Suddenly, he felt as though he were gazing at his own reflection. So, he was not the only one who felt restless and dissatisfied in Rekova Valley. "Do you think you'll ever get back to the coast?"

Tom's broad shoulders rose and fell in a brief shrug. "Maybe someday. But now I belong here. My family needs all of us to help." He began to sand the boat frame again with great industry. "This valley isn't so bad. Greener, nicer than some."

Rubbing the sandpaper over the wood, Mark's mind was busy with what he'd just heard. Tom was making the best of doing what he didn't really want to do, of staying where he had no desire to stay. *My family needs my help.* Mark shook off a little twinge that nipped at him. After all, Tom probably had no other choice — he had to stay. But Mark was luckier, he could leave. Yet he couldn't make himself tell this new friend that he was soon escaping from the valley. "Yes, it is a pretty place," he agreed. That much, at least, was true.

Then he found himself talking to Tom at great length about Otsego Falls and Chuck Wilson and their baseball team, the Otters.

"Ralph likes baseball!" Tom exclaimed, stopping his work for a moment. "He's good at it. Now you two can be friends."

Mark said nothing, but he felt that it wouldn't be as easy as that to make friends with surly Ralph Bates.

"Tomorrow, we'll put on the first coat of shellac," Tom said, looking proudly at the boat frame. "When that's dry, we'll put on one more." He turned to Mark. "Thanks for helping me."

"I'd like to help with the rest of it, too," Mark offered. He'd enjoyed this day more than any he'd spent so far in Rekova Valley, not counting the hunting and fishing expeditions with his father. When he came home to dinner, he knew that Dad was pleased that he'd made a friend here at last.

But it still wasn't like home. After dinner, Mark began writing a letter to Chuck, gratefully accepting the family's offer. He knew that his father would correspond with Mrs. Wilson, making all necessary arrangements.

Soon, Mark's pen stopped moving as his mind began to
dwell on Chuck's warm companionship and on the com-
forts of Chuck's attractive big house. For a long while,
Mark sat there, dreaming. At length, he folded the
unfinished letter and went up to the loft. He'd complete
the letter and mail it when he found out the one
necessary fact that remained — the date of his flight
home with Greg. Before he got ready for bed, Mark
folded and stacked some of his clothing. This preparation
for packing made the anticipated journey seem closer.

"Ruthie really loves my doll," he heard Lynn telling
their father. "Sometime I'm going to let her keep Sally
Sue over the weekend. Sally Sue, will you be a good
girl while you're visiting Ruth?"

Mark could picture his sister earnestly addressing her
doll, as though it were human.

"The little Indian girl is a nice friend." Dad's voice
floated up. "Your teacher told me that some years ago
the Athabascans used to lead a gypsy life, moving
around with the seasons. But now most of them cooperate
with the compulsory school attendance law. They stay
in the community all year so that their children won't
miss school."

"I'm glad Ruth lives here all the time. We have fun
together. She's lucky," Lynn declared. "She gets to ride
in their boat a lot."

"Yes, the river is their road."

Mark fell asleep as the voices murmured on.

Every spare moment that Mark and Tom Anahuk had
was spent working on the boat, while big, snowy Ilik
watched them. Sunny weather dried the two coats of
shellac to shiny hardness. "See what my friend Joe gave

me in exchange for a big fish catch." Tom showed
Mark a good-sized waterproof tarp. "This is our canvas,
old but in good shape."

Putting the canvas over the wooden boat skeleton
was a hard, tedious job. Slowly and with care, the boys
applied glue and pounded in countless tacks along the
seams. After three days' steady work, the canvas was at
last stretched tautly over the frame, and except for the
finishing touches, the boat was now complete. Mark felt
a stir of pride at the part he'd played in creating the
canoe's neat, trim appearance.

"Now we'll grease her with linseed oil," Tom said.
Mark discovered that the Eskimo boy had earned oil
and paint by doing odd jobs during the summer in the
Rekova general store.

"How would you like to come to my house for a while
today?" Tom asked, when they'd finished that afternoon's work.

Mark agreed. They were lucky enough to get a ride
in one of the lumber trucks. Mark had never seen where
the few Eskimo families lived. When he first came to
Alaska, he'd pictured Eskimos living in winter igloos
made of snow blocks, but his father told him that this
was done only in emergencies or for temporary shelter.
"The igloos I've seen were made of scrap lumber and
logs, combined with metal sheets made from oil cans,"
Dad recalled. "The huts were then banked with sod
blocks for insulation. In summer, canvas tents were
popular with some groups." Mark knew that here in the
valley, Eskimos lived in log houses like his own and
that most of the men worked in the sawmill as his
father did.

When he got off the truck with Tom, Mark saw several cabins nestled in the fold of a low foothill, snugly sheltered from any winds that winter might bring. The houses seemed to be bursting with grown-ups of all ages and many merry-faced children. Tom's brothers and sisters excitedly made Mark welcome. Several of the smaller ones were playing a game of Yo-Yo, rapidly twirling two small fur balls attached to leather strings. When Mark admired their skill, they urged him to try it. He found it very hard to make the two balls revolve in opposite directions at the same time, to the great amusement of the little Eskimos. More noise broke out as the barks of a pack of handsome husky dogs were added to the greetings.

"Lynn would love those huskies," Mark remarked.

"When some of ours have pups we'll save your sister a nice one," Tom offered.

Inside the house, Tom's mother, plump and cheerful, sat busily rolling wirelike strands in her hands. "Happy to meet my son's good friend." She nodded and smiled to Mark, who looked with interest at what she was doing.

"My mother's making thread of caribou sinew, to sew skins," Tom explained. "For gloves, parkas, dog-harness straps. This thread will never break."

Mark watched her roll the thin, damp strands rapidly back and forth as Eskimo women had done for centuries, first in her hands and then against her cheekbone, over and over so that they united into one strong thread.

"Time for *kupiak* now," the woman said, and Mark was surprised to smell coffee brewing. A smiling, gnome-like little woman, who turned out to be Tom's grand-

mother, served the hot coffee around. She had a
wrinkled, venerable face and hands like curled brown
leaves.

A little later, Tom's mother brought forward a pair
of new fur boots. "No mukluks your size," she said.
Mark nodded, grinning. Eskimos never had feet as
large as his. "But my son say these fit your sister. Good
for winter."

"Gosh, thanks." Mark accepted the boots for Lynn.
They were made of hide with the furry side out. The
top part was artistically decorated in a geometric design
with colored yarns, and Mark noticed warm innersoles
of dried grasses.

"My mother makes the best mukluks of anybody," said
the Eskimo proudly. "Look —" Tom pointed to where
the tough mukluk soles were crimped to fit heels and
toes. "In the old days, women used to shape the soles
by biting the leather with their teeth. Now for this job
most of them use pliers, like my mother." He also showed
Mark the *ulu*, which was a very sharp homemade knife
with a single blade. Mark learned that this was an
Eskimo woman's most useful and important tool.

That evening at dinner, Mark told his father all about
the visit, remarking on the contrast of the old and the
new in Eskimo life. Tom's winter parka would be made
of skins that had been trapped, tanned and sewn by
the family, Mark mused. Every step of the garment's
creation, from elusive animal to warm hooded jacket,
would be done in the timeworn way. Yet Tom's summer
jacket was a Sears mail-order blue denim with a zipper,
similar to Mark's.

"The ancient, side by side with the modern." Dad

nodded. "Primitive boats — with roaring outboard motors attached to them. Aged natives, traveling from outpost to town — not by dogsled as you might imagine, but by plane. The Eskimos are hardy and resourceful, Mark, with a strong sense of fun. They are people who can adapt themselves to changing patterns of life. Some advances in the native way of life are good," Dad went on, "but many of the Eskimo customs are very sound. Not all the old habits and arts should be changed."

Lynn, seated nearby, held up her feet in the new fur boots and admired them for the hundredth time. But she was even more thrilled by the promise of a lively husky pup some future day.

The next sunshiny weekend, Mark and Tom worked again on the boat, giving her two coats of good white paint. "What are you going to name her?" Mark asked, stepping back to admire the results of their labor. The topic of names reminded him of Dad's words about how native Indian and Eskimo first names had all but disappeared in favor of Christian names learned from early missionaries.

Tom, cleaning the brushes, pondered the question. "*Tara-i-tua-luk* — he who is without shadow," he said at last. "That is the great polar bear, Mark. He is like part of the land, as he stands almost unseen against the snow."

"The *Polar Bear*. That's good!" Mark agreed.

"No real polar bears around here, of course." Tom smiled. "Still, I like that name. Say, you're a good printer. Will you paint the name on her tomorrow?" As Mark nodded, Tom frowned at the few narrow boards he

had left. "These aren't wide enough for paddles. Joe
at the sawmill might have the right size. I'll ask him
tomorrow." He looked with pride at the boat. "When
the paint's dry, we'll put in two seats and try her out.
Did you ever paddle a board, Mark?"

"A little, when we had a canoe at the lake one
vacation."

With the boards, Tom showed Mark the right way
to stroke, as they stood in the birch grove. "This is how
you guide a canoe through the current. But it feels
different in the water," Tom admitted, as Mark made a
few practice strokes through the air.

You'd really have to know what you were doing on
the big Wolverine, Mark thought, glancing at the rolling
river. He threw down the boards as Tom unchained
Ilik and they started for home.

The next day while Tom was at the sawmill, Mark
walked down alone to the riverbank to paint the name
on the *Polar Bear* with a cardboard stencil he'd made.
The boat was turned upside down on two stumps,
smooth and glistening white as an ice pack in the sun.
Mark touched his fingers to the hull and was pleased
to feel that the paint was bone-dry. He was just about
to open the can of paint for the name, when he heard
a sharp, sudden cry from the river. Mark ran down to
the water's edge. He gasped to see a figure in a flat-
bottomed boat poling desperately to avoid the big fallen
spruce tree across the river. Mark stared. It was Ralph
Bates!

As Mark watched in alarm, the clumsy boat struck
the half-submerged tree and tipped over sideways.
Ralph Bates seized the nearest drooping branches of the

fallen tree and hung on. The Wolverine's swift current spun his boat away from the tree's limbs, and it sped downstream. Mark's heartbeats quickened as he saw Ralph try to reach a more secure position. The dripping boy worked his way to the slippery log tree trunk and clung there. Deep, angry water swirled all around him. The rocky bank, unmarked by footholds, rose steeply behind him. To swim ashore in that icy surge would be impossible. Ralph Bates was stranded.

Mark turned to run home for help. Then he realized in dismay that his father was working today. The sawmill was too far away to get anyone quickly. He looked out in anxiety at the quiet road. Not a passerby was in sight. It might be a long time — hours — before anyone would happen along. By that time, Ralph Bates would be so chilled and exhausted that he might easily slip from his dangerous perch.

Mark took a deep breath. Somehow, he would have to get Ralph out of the glacial river himself. But how — how? If only he had some strong rope. Mark looked around in desperation. The boat — Tom Anahuk's boat. Mark's muscles tensed. There was no other way. He would have to try it.

Ralph had seen him and was calling to him in shrill urgency. "Bennett! Bennett! Get help!"

Mark waved to show that he'd heard, and then he began to tug the *Polar Bear* off the stumps and down to the river's edge. The boat weighed over a hundred pounds, and Mark's breath came in panting gasps. As he went back for the two boards that Tom had said were too narrow for paddles, Mark tried to remember what the Eskimo boy had told him. He pushed away

the nervousness that surged over him, but he couldn't
help wishing that he'd had a few lessons in the canoe.

Mark tried to think clearly. He dropped the boards
into the canoe. How far it looked across the stretch of
strong water to where Ralph crouched in fright upon
the fallen log. Mark must start from upstream, because
the current would carry him down. And he would have
to approach the log with great care, so that he wouldn't
tip over or let the boat be pierced by sharp branches.

Mark's heart thumped as he set the *Polar Bear* in
dead water behind a big rock. He got into it and knelt
down in the center. Slowly, he paddled out with one
of the boards, trying to recall Tom's advice. Oh, the
Wolverine's current was strong! The *Polar Bear* leaped
forward, and Mark had to stroke with all his might so
that he wouldn't get swept past Ralph. There — out to
the center. So far, so good. Mark felt like a cork bobbing
on top of the coursing brown-green water. He tried not
to think of its depth, its force. He must concentrate
only on reaching that tree, whose deep roots held it
firm.

Ralph's voice seemed calm and free of panic, as he
shouted directions to Mark. "Hold it steady! A little to
the right. Come on, easy."

Mark's fear began to fade, too. The worst was over.
He was going to make it. He saw how he could pull
in beside the fallen tree trunk, so that the trapped boy
could get into the boat. Then they would paddle back
to shore together.

Suddenly, Ralph's voice, raw with fright, yelled a
warning to him. "Look out, Bennett! The logs!"

Mark glanced over his shoulder. His breath caught

in his throat. Half a dozen big logs — runaways from
the sawmill — came charging down the crest of the
river, churning the water white. He was directly in their
path as they surged forward — heavy battering rams that
could smash Tom's light boat to bits!

12

FRIENDSHIP

"Quick!" Ralph shouted. "Head for the tree!"

Mark paddled furiously, forcing the canoe out of the main current. He felt the strong pull of the river beneath him as the boat slid past the fallen spruce tree. Oh, he mustn't let himself get swept downstream! Mark strained at the paddle with all his strength. Slowly, slowly, the *Polar Bear* turned into the eddying water at the lower side of the fallen tree. Mark gasped with relief.

Ralph, clinging to the tree trunk with one arm, seized the edge of the boat with his other hand. Mark, still kneeling in the canoe, grabbed a tree limb. Between them, they held the boat securely. And not a moment too soon! A booming jar shook the half-submerged tree as one of the logs hit against it. The log bounced out again to the middle of the river.

Mark's heart thudded rapidly. He'd just made it. Another few seconds and that heavy log would have hit him. Another log banged against the tree and shook it, and another. How lucky it was that Mark had gotten in *behind* the big tree. It now acted as a buffer against the dangerous logs.

Ralph clung to the quivering trunk, and Mark clutched the branch. Then the last of the heavy logs were gone, zigzagging crazily down the Wolverine. "That was close!" Ralph gasped. Mark was too shaken to reply.

Cautiously, Ralph inched himself into the *Polar Bear* and picked up one of the boards that lay on the bottom. "I was going downstream to fish," he said. "All at once the rowboat got out of control."

Mark let go of the limb, and the canoe slid into midstream. They steadily plied the makeshift oars. What a difference it made with two people rowing. The *Polar Bear* cut easily across the river, coming ashore just below the spot where Tom had built her. Mark shivered. He was as wet from spray as Ralph was from his dunking. Together, they dragged the boat up the mossy bank.

"Lucky it wasn't our motorboat that I lost," Ralph confided. "Then I'd really get it. But I don't think my father will be too mad at me for losing that old scow."

Mark's eyes narrowed. Wasn't Ralph even going to thank him for the risk he'd taken? Mark knelt down and examined long black marks along the *Polar Bear*'s hull. He was glad to see that they were only on the surface. "She's not torn." He gave a sigh of relief as he straightened up. Tom's boat had passed her first test nobly.

"A good little boat," Ralph admitted, as though reading Mark's mind. "Say, I'd — uh — like to help paint her again, if you and Tom will let me."

Mark turned around, surprised not only by Ralph's words, but by the tone. Was that humble voice really coming from big, aggressive Ralph Bates? Ralph stood uncertainly, looking everywhere except at Mark. In a sudden flash of insight, Mark knew how hard it was for Ralph to give in, even this little bit.

"Sure," Mark said. "Tom has some paint left."

They carried the boat back to the birch grove. How much lighter she felt with someone sharing the load.

"Bennett —" Ralph cleared his throat, " — uh — thanks for getting me off the log."

Now that thanks had been expressed, Mark felt uncomfortable and at a loss for words. He looked down at the ground, where drops from their soaked clothing made dark little polka dots as they stood there. In a moment, the thought came to him that Ralph Bates lived much too far away to go home in those wet clothes. "Come to my place and change. You can put on some things of mine."

"Okay."

They walked in silence out of the woods and down the double rut leading to the Bennetts' house. Suddenly, Ralph spoke again. "Tom was right. You're not afraid. I never thought for a minute you'd come after me yourself."

Mark shrugged, embarrassed by this praise. "I would've got help, but there wasn't time."

"Bennett," Ralph swallowed, then stumbled on. "At school, you made me mad, acting like a big-city snob." He hesitated. "I'm sorry. About ganging up on you, and everything."

"Forget it," Mark mumbled. He could sense Ralph's

uncomfortable feeling. Apologizing came very hard to
people like Ralph. *And like me,* Mark thought with quick
honesty. So he and Ralph Bates were alike, in at least
one respect. Mark's memory went back to his first day
at school. "I guess I had a pretty big chip on my
shoulder," he said. "Bates," Mark abruptly changed the
subject, "Tom said you like baseball. So do I. After we
change our clothes, let's hit a few."

Ralph eagerly agreed.

"Hey, what happened?" Lynn's eyes grew round as
she met them. Mark explained briefly and then asked
where their father was. "Not home from work yet?"

"No. Miss Elliott just drove me back. She's starting a
junior arts and crafts class at her house."

After Ralph and Mark had changed, Lynn joined them
in having drinks of canned fruit juice and crusty slices
of bread, spread thickly with Mrs. Lewis' wild berry
jam. Then, they went out in front of the house to play
ball.

"Lynn, will you help field them?" Mark called out.
He'd go easy on Ralph. An Alaskan farm boy couldn't
compete with someone who had played in county
leagues.

"You want to bat first?" Ralph asked.

"All right."

Ralph wound up while Mark waited. Like a shot, the
ball whizzed past. Wow! Ralph had really got off a
lucky one. Mark gripped his bat. But Ralph's next pitch
zipped past with equal speed, although Mark swung
heavily at it.

"Stri-i-ke two!" Lynn shrieked, as she plunged into
the wild grass after the ball. Mark gave her a dark

look. "You've played before, Ralph?" he asked.

"I pitched at school in Ketchikan for a while before we moved up here," Ralph said, pounding his fist into the glove Mark had loaned him. "Once we started a team here in the valley. Called it the Malemutes. But it folded up when some boys moved away."

So, Ralph had some pitching experience. Well, after Mark hit a few, Ralph could take his turn at bat and see how a real pitcher operated. Again Mark faced Ralph, and again he struck empty air. A grudging admiration began to blend with his surprise. Ralph was good, very good, and he didn't even seem to realize it. Mark tried hard, but aside from some foul tips and a little blooper, he couldn't get a hit off Ralph.

Then, they changed places. What was the matter with Mark's curve ball? He couldn't get it across the way he wanted. High, wide. Ah, there was a good one that fooled Ralph. But dissatisfaction gnawed at Mark. Out of practice, that's what the trouble was. He hadn't played for so long.

Stormy's barks announced that Dad was coming home. George Bennett looked curiously at Ralph, squeezed into Mark's pants and printed sport shirt, which were a size too small for him. Dad's face clouded with concern when he heard about their adventure on the river. But Mark could tell that his father was proud of him and happy that he had made another friend.

As he walked to the gate with Ralph, discontent nagged at Mark. What a waste it was for Ralph to have that natural speed and coordination. Mark wished desperately that he possessed it instead. With his trick curve, what a combination it would be. There wouldn't

be a hitter who could touch him. Pitcher was the only
position Mark liked to play. The pitcher was the main-
spring of a team — vital, important.

"Hey, Bennett, I have something I want to give you."
Ralph swung his bundle of wet clothes. "It's a totem
pole."

A toy totem pole? Mark had seen them being sold
for souvenirs back in Fairbanks. Ralph probably felt that
he owed Mark something for getting him out of the river.
But Mark didn't want anything — least of all, one of
those ugly little totems. Mark shook his head.

"I want to," Ralph insisted. "I'll bring it over someday." He began to speak again of the Malemutes, the
baseball team that he had tried to keep going in
Rekova Valley. "It was no use. Not enough guys. I
really liked it down on the Panhandle," he disclosed,
kicking at a rock in his path. "We had a good gang of
fellows, and there were always sports or other things to
do."

First, Tom Anahuk, Mark thought in surprise — now
Ralph. And Mark had thought he was the only one
who had to leave well-loved scenes and friends behind.

On Monday morning, Miss Elliott beamed to see the
three big boys at peace with one another.

"It must have been hard on the teacher to have us
fighting," Mark said at recess.

Ralph and Tom nodded. "She's a nice lady." The
Eskimo boy's voice was warm. Everyone in the valley
liked Miss Elliott, Mark reflected, and he could easily
see why.

When he came home that afternoon, Lynn met him.
She had already run into the house and changed into

blue jeans. As she ran toward him, her braids shook with excitement. "Guess what, Mark? Daddy got a letter from the Hillmans. They're coming to visit us on Saturday!"

Company, in the little house on Eagle Road. Mark was pleased that there would be some change in their routine. "It'll be nice to see them again." He liked the family with whom they had traveled to Alaska. He wondered how Tim and Donna were, and if their parents were having any luck with the farm in Crescent Valley. Mark's father gave him their letter to read. The Hillmans had written that they would pay a call before winter snowed everybody in.

Mark walked to the window and gazed out. Nature was getting ready for the change of season. Many birds had winged southward. Animals were preparing for the cold weather in various ways. Soon, the severe winter would turn this green and golden valley into white desolation. Other changes would take place. The hunters would be gone, and the sawmill workers. And before freeze-up, Mark would be gone, too.

The next morning as Mark waited for the bus with Lynn, a sawmill truck groaned to a stop beside them. Ralph Bates jumped down from the cab and called out, "Give me a hand, Bennett!"

Ralph began to pull a pole from atop the load of logs. Mark, helping him, saw that it was a carved totem. Suddenly, he remembered. Oh, no! Not that hideous thing.

Ralph tugged at it, and together they got it off the truck. The driver waved good-bye and drove on. "Let's put it on your property, so it'll be safe," Ralph said.

As if anybody would want to steal that witch doctor's nightmare, Mark thought.

It was about 10 feet long and more slender than some Mark had seen. As they carried it through the gate, Lynn hopped around like a wound-up jumping jack. They laid the totem pole at the side of the lane, face up. Mark thought he had never seen anything more grotesque than those big carved faces at such close range.

"It's cedar," Ralph said proudly. "Made by the Tlingit Indians." Ralph pronounced the name *Klink' et.* "An Indian in the Panhandle gave it to me three years ago, when I found his little boy who was lost in the woods."

Ralph was so proud of that awful totem pole. Mark didn't know what to say. "Did the Indians believe these — things kept evil spirits away?" he managed to ask.

"No. This totem was like a family tree, tracing the family's history. Some tribes kept the totem outside the doorway. This one's just the right size for a marker by your gate. Look," Ralph went on eagerly, "it suits your family. See the big bird on top, like a raven with its wings out? Well, that could mean your father. Someday he might have his own plane. Lots of Alaskans do."

"Hey, that funny animal face could be Stormy!" Lynn cried. "And the little spooky face at the bottom could mean me."

"Sure. And see this fish? A salmon, who travels far. *You* traveled far to get to this valley, Mark. See?"

"Here comes the bus!" Lynn shouted, and they hurried out to the road again.

"Thanks, Ralph," Mark murmured dubiously, as they got on the bus. He wished he knew how to refuse the gift. As long as he lived here, he was never going to put that weird collection of Halloween masks by their gate.

"We have our own totem pole now!" Lynn chattered loudly to Miss Elliott in the school yard. "With our family's —" she paused, searching for the word.

"Crest? Coat of arms?" the smiling teacher helped out.

Lynn vigorously nodded. "Ralph gave it to Mark, because he saved him from drowning."

Why couldn't she keep still? Mark felt uncomfortable as Miss Elliott gazed at him. "I heard about the courageous rescue, Mark."

"Ralph wasn't really drowning." Mark glared at Lynn. "Besides, if Tom's boat hadn't been there, I couldn't have done anything."

Miss Elliott didn't press the point. "I'm glad you're getting on well with the boys in the valley," she said gently. "Ralph must think a lot of you to part with that Tlingit totem pole."

That big old pile of odd figures? Mark looked at her, puzzled.

"I know that Ralph treasured it," the teacher said. "The Bates boys have few belongings of their own. The family has had a hard struggle getting their farm going because of sickness and other misfortunes. It was inconvenient to carry that totem along when they moved up here. But Ralph's parents let him bring it, because totems are rather rare and it meant so much to him." She hurried off to ring the bell.

Mark followed slowly while mixed emotions stirred around inside him. All morning, his mind kept wandering from his studies. Tom and Ralph had offered him their friendship, not with empty words, but with what each loved best — sharing a skill, giving a dearly beloved possession.

At lunch hour, as the three boys played catch, Ralph said, "I wish we could get the Malemutes going again. But there aren't enough boys our age in the valley to form a team."

Every time they played ball, Mark marveled at how fast Ralph was. Maybe with a great deal of practice Mark could work up his own speed. He'd always been so proud of his curve ball that it felt strange to meet someone who could pitch just as well. No, Mark admitted reluctantly to himself, not just as well — better. And the funny part of it was that Ralph didn't even recognize his own talent.

"Get a team together next year when you go to high school in Rekova," Tom said. "There'll be enough boys there."

"Would you be on the high school team, too?" Mark asked.

"They'd only take me if they needed players real bad," Tom admitted cheerfully. "I'm not very good at baseball. But what I'd like is a chance to go to workshop class. I saw it once in Setnek, boys learning about tractors, aircraft engines, diesels."

"Tom's a born mechanic," Ralph declared. "I saw him take more than one outboard motor apart, fix it and put it back together so it worked like new."

Mark could well believe it. He knew how willing and clever those brown hands of Tom's were. He'd heard that many of the Eskimos had natural ability with machines. Dad told him that some of them had become skilled technicians on the Distant Early Warning line,

the great string of arctic radar stations known as the
DEW line.

Mark's mind was crowded with new thoughts of his
Alaskan friends. Ralph and Tom, with some of their
strange ways, seemed so different from a person like
Chuck Wilson. And yet were they really different? They
had dreams and hopes, fears and joys, like anyone else.
Mark gazed across the school yard, his mind restless and
confused. When the bell called them inside, he could
not concentrate on his books, but found himself staring
out the window, thinking of many things.

That afternoon, Mark asked his father to help him
dig a deep hole by the gate in which to set the big
totem pole. He had decided, after all, that he couldn't
hurt Ralph's feelings.

"Let's paint it with bright colors," Lynn proposed. "I
want my little face on it to have green eyes, a red
mouth and big white teeth, so it'll look fiercer."

"We'll see." Dad gave her braid a tug.

Mark stood looking at the carved totem after his father
and sister had gone back to the cabin. There was the
big bird on top, with its wings outspread. And here
was the salmon who had traveled far. The totem looked
different. It had a certain dignity. Maybe it was because
it now stood up straight and tall. Mark walked slowly
to the house, deep in thought. It was strange — even
the cabin looked better, snug and cozy against its background of wild beauty.

13

DECISION

The Bennetts were kept busy on Saturday fixing a good meal for the Hillmans, who were expected to arrive about three o'clock. Tasty big mushrooms and cranberries, which Mark and Lynn had picked the previous day, were prepared. George Bennett had hung the mallard ducks he'd bagged on sharp stakes, so that they'd be drained and chilled, ready for the oven, while he bought some groceries in Rekova.

Miss Elliott was invited and came over early in the afternoon to help. Later, as she took two big juicy blueberry pies from the oven, the sound of a car was heard. Everyone hurried outside in the crisp air.

"It's the Hillmans!" Lynn cried. There stood the familiar cream-colored station wagon that had carried Mark and Lynn from Otsego Falls. "Hi, Stormy's boy, Stormy's girl!" called little Donna, as her mother lifted her out.

"She can say *s* now," Tim Hillman proudly announced.

Stormy happily nuzzled Donna and Tim and everybody talked at once. "Here's Dad!" George Bennett had returned from his errand just in time.

"Come inside," he invited. "Jean," he said to Miss Elliott, "I'd like you to meet our friends, John and Amy Hillman. This is Jean Elliott."

"George has told me so much about you," the teacher said.

Mark looked in surprise from his father to Miss Elliott. Her gray eyes glowed, and Dad's face looked bright and happy. They had called each other by their first names, and it sounded nice. Funny, but Mark had never before given a thought to the fact that grown-ups could be lonely, too.

As the Hillmans got seated by the fire, Dad took Mark aside for a moment. "Mark, here's the news you've been waiting for. In Rekova, I just got word from Greg. The flight's all set." Mark noticed that a tight line suddenly appeared around his father's mouth. "You'll leave at the end of the month."

Mark nodded, wondering why he didn't feel happier at this news. Was it because, with all these people around, he couldn't think straight?

"That's a splendid totem at your gate," John Hillman said. "But when I saw it, I thought surely we had the wrong farm." He turned to Mark. "You used to think totems were ugly. Did you change your mind about them, Mark?"

"Yes," Mark admitted, "after I found out what they meant."

Mr. Hillman nodded. "That's true about many things in life. We often dislike what we don't understand."

"It's cedar," Mark said with pride. "Carved by the

Tlingit Indians." Mr. Hillman was right. It was a magnificent totem pole.

The log house was really too small to hold so much company, but no one seemed to mind. Miss Elliott moved quietly from stove to table, serving the meal. There were baked potatoes, biscuits, roast duck with mushrooms and cranberry sauce, and for dessert, blueberry pie.

Mark decided that he liked Miss Elliott's presence in the house. When she was here, everything seemed complete. He remembered with pleasure how attractively she could fix up a plain log cabin.

The evening sped by with a lively flow of talk, the firelight making dancing shadows on all their faces. Somewhat to Mark's discomfiture, the conversation came around to his rescue of Ralph Bates on the Wolverine. The Hillmans were so impressed that Mark was relieved when at length the subject changed.

The visitors were greatly interested in George Bennett's plans for his land, and Dad in turn asked many questions about their venture. They had started a dairy farm in the Crescent Valley with a small holstein herd. John Hillman worked part-time in a store in town to earn money for feed and farm equipment.

"In spite of short grazing seasons and long barn-bound winters, Alaskan cows yield good quantities of milk," he told them. "Few pests bother them in this climate, although we've had a little trouble with marauding brown bears."

Dan Towers and his wife had claimed a vegetable farm to the south of Crescent Valley and had great hopes for its future success. "Pandowdy, the dog, is as mischievous as ever," Mrs. Hillman related. "I think the Alaskan climate has made his appetite sharper and his tricks bolder."

Little Donna, holding Sally Sue, fell asleep in her mother's arms. "Lynn, I was just thinking —" Miss Elliott looked at the little girl with the doll. "I have pieces of cloth left from sewing and some yellow yarn. During the long winter nights how would you like to help me make two more rag dolls?"

Lynn clapped her hands. "Yes, let's! And I bet I know who they're for. Donna and Ruthie."

The teacher smiled. "Right. Go to the head of the class."

All too soon, it was time to go. Miss Elliott invited the visitors to spend the night at her house, since she had more room. They thanked her and agreed. Before starting back for their distant valley next day, they planned to see the Bennetts once more.

"Gee, how lucky you are to sleep up there." Tim Hillman pointed longingly to Mark's attic as the grown-ups said good night. "What a neat little room, with its own ladder and everything. I wish I had one like that. I'd play I was a pirate."

Mark had an idea. "Would you like to sleep there tonight on my bunk? I could use a sleeping bag."

Tim's eyes danced. "Oh, Mom, Daddy, can I?"

"Okay, Captain Kidd," his father said, "as long as Mark is willing."

The Bennetts waved good-bye from their porch as the station wagon and Miss Elliott's car jogged their way out to the road. "It's been a busy day," George Bennett said as they came indoors. Lynn went sleepily to bed with her doll. Tim Hillman was already halfway up the ladder.

"Good night, Dad." Mark climbed to the loft, where he found Tim looking out of the window, no doubt imagining that he was in the crow's nest of a buccaneer galleon and that the fields outside were rolling seas.

Mark went over and stood silently beside the little boy, gazing out where the mountain's bulk guarded the shadowy valley. A strange feeling gripped him. Dad's land was out there — *his* land, too — waiting to be tamed, to be coaxed into producing crops. This was no place for weaklings. To wrest a living from new soil meant hard work and battles with the elements. It would be a rugged life. But would it really be such a lonely one?

Dad had said that a man could become anything he wanted here. A pilot, serving remote villages. A doctor, like the Lewises' son. An engineer, building roads and bridges in the wilderness.

Tim Hillman started to get ready for bed. "Gosh, you're brave, Mark!" he sighed in a worshipful tone. "Saving that shipwrecked boy from drowning! That's the bravest thing I ever heard."

Brave. Mark's face flushed in the dim lamplight. Brave indeed. If little Tim only knew. Was it brave to walk out on your family because things didn't go the way you wanted? Did it take courage to run away from work and problems?

Mark tucked the small boy into his bunk. He looked at his pile of belongings, ready to be packed into suitcases bound for Otsego Falls. Long after Tim had fallen asleep, Mark still sat by the window. Bright streamers of the aurora borealis began to flash and dance across the sky. Soon, snow would start flying thickly and the tawny Wolverine would be locked beneath an armor of ice. Dad and Lynn would bundle themselves into fur-lined parkas, and indoors the Yukon stove would burn cheerily.

But Mark wouldn't be here for any of it, because he had chosen a different life. He took out the letter he'd written to Chuck Wilson, the letter that was now ready to be completed and mailed.

Thanks a million for your family's offer, he read to himself. *Boy, you're saving my life! Will I be glad to get back home to Otsego Falls! You don't know what this awful place is like. The boys around here have never been anyplace or seen anything, and the school is nothing like Madison —*

Mark read no more, because suddenly he knew the answer to all the confusion that had filled his mind in recent days. Home. Otsego Falls was Chuck's home. But it was no longer Mark's. Home meant being with your own, to help, to strengthen, to belong. To share — the good and the bad. To give and take. To love.

Mark knew now that he wanted to ride behind lead-dog Ilik and the husky team some white winter day. He wanted to share in the excitement of the big ice breakup in the spring and to watch the midnight base-ball game with his father on a June night in Fairbanks. But most of all, he wanted to see how this valley looked when it was waving in grain.

With quick, sure strokes Mark tore the letter in half.

Dear Chuck, he wrote on a fresh piece of paper, *Thanks a million for your family's kind offer, but I won't be coming back. The truth is I like it here now, and*